Accidental Damage

'Tales from the house that sat down'

Book 1

By

Alice May

with love
Alice May
x

Alice May

Copyright

Acknowledgements

There are a number of people without whom this story would never have seen the light of day.

Therefore I would like to take this opportunity to thank my neighbour Nelly for suggesting that I write this book. I also thank my parents, my daughters and my good friend Catherine for being extremely patient and reading the very earliest drafts. Your comments have been very gratefully received.

After that I must thank my fellow author H. T. King for the excellent advice and encouragement and also my wonderful editor Rose King.

Thanks also to mnsartstudio, I absolutely love what you have done with my original painting for the cover design.

In addition I would like to thank both my parents and my parents-in-law for all their support throughout the events that inspired this story. I don't know what we would have done without you.

Finally, of course, I thank my Beloved Husband for everything. x

For my Beloved Husband and the Barbarians

Contents

PART 1

'No one saves us but ourselves.
No one can and no one may.
We ourselves must walk the path.'

Buddha

Alice May

<u>Preamble</u>

Definition: a preliminary statement by the author to the reader

Please allow me to introduce you to our heroine.

Unfortunately I am forced to admit that she is not at her best at the moment. An honest raconteur would tell you that, in fact, she is a complete mess.

However, that is rather the point of this tale!

There is the mother of all tempests raging outside and she is trying to pretend that she is not absolutely petrified. (Between you and me, she is not hiding it terribly well.) As a person who does not know her, you would be forgiven for thinking that she is a bit of a wimp.

You are entitled to your opinion of course, but perhaps you might consider giving her the benefit of the doubt. After all, she remembers being a very different person.

There was a time when she was a strong and confident individual and found such squalls exhilarating. She remembers running along a beach in Spain one stormy night (more years ago now than she cares to recall) hand in hand with the love of her life, drenched with heavy rain, laughing as angry waves snatched at their ankles while thunder and lightning cascaded down around them shattering the darkness.

In short, she used to love storms.

Alice May

Once upon a time she felt indestructible. Sadly our heroine cannot claim to possess such an indomitable spirit anymore. That person is gone.

What on earth happened?

You might well ask!

There are countless ways that hearts can break and now, when the lightning flashes and the thunder roars, our heroine jumps in terror. She tries valiantly to pretend that she is not hiding away and whimpering quietly deep inside herself like a wounded animal. Unable to rest she paces her home from room to room looking for somewhere safe to hide, searching desperately for something to divert her attention so that she can ignore what is happening outside.

Today, she is in luck! Something fairly momentous is about to happen to her which will distract her completely from the stupendous meteorological conditions currently stomping around.

She is about to revisit the past.

I will leave her to tell you all about it, now.

After all, it is her story, not mine.

1: <u>Compulsion</u>
Definition: an irresistible impulse to act.

Present day....

It was late in the evening on a seriously scary, stormy night when I finally had to admit to myself that I was a wreck.

A well-known pop diva was letting rip at full volume from the radio in the corner (a vain attempt on my part to drown out the noise from outside). Yet, I was still jumping with fright at each new flash of lightning and then again for the subsequent growling thunder.

As the aforementioned diva vociferously queried the whereabouts of all the more admirable gentlemen in the world, a small part of my brain was muttering, resentfully, that they were all probably comfortably ensconced in the lounge, watching the football with a tinny, like my Beloved Husband, and having a fine old time without us both.

Nevertheless, as the wind howled and the rain pulverised the ground (and the diva continued to lament at length), there I was, a fully grown woman, cowering in the kitchen. I really couldn't pretend anymore. I knew, without a shadow of a doubt, that it was high time I sorted myself out and in order to do that I needed to find something, or, more accurately, a box of somethings.

This sudden compulsion to take action was unexpectedly and entirely overwhelming. It was so all-consuming that it made the noises of the storm, and even the deafening diva, fade into insignificance.

Incapable of preventing myself, I left the kitchen at speed and dived headfirst into the dark and dangerous space that constituted the *under-stairs cupboard* in a desperate attempt to excavate long buried treasures. Things that had once been so important to a previous 'me', things that I had since told myself I wanted nothing more to do with. Ever!

In spite of my dogged assertion that I was done with them, these gems had somehow been spared the destructive fires of two years previously, when so much of the old 'me' was deliberately and systematically obliterated. I had stood in the darkness back then, completely devoid of all emotion, watching as so many things I had loved were engulfed in the heat and crackle of dancing flames.

Yet, secretly packaged away in the deepest darkest space I could find, these select items had been purposefully forgotten.

A line had been drawn. A door closed.

That part of my life was over.

Well, until now obviously!

The urge to be reunited with them immediately was so strong that I was heedless of the potential threat from the enormous eight legged occupants, the presence of which usually prevented me from venturing very far into this uncharted territory.

Out came old sleeping bags, wellies of assorted sizes and a plethora of ancient coats and shoes that I vaguely

Accidental Damage

recognised as having been worn at some point by one or other of the smaller humans that roam through the house from time to time in search of food and electronic entertainment.

Right at the back was the box. I dragged it out eagerly, notwithstanding the unwieldy size and sheer weight of it, and pulled it right across the hall into the little study, oblivious to the trail of abandoned detritus that I was leaving in my wake.

At last I had them.

Nothing else mattered.

Opening the box, I released my treasures, carefully extracting one thing after another. Each item unearthed generated a tingle down my spine, a spark of recognition, a brief flash of the person I used to be, as I cautiously arranged them on the desk by the window.

Time passed. I was so utterly enthralled that I did not notice when the storm outside had blown itself out. I did not even register that the radio had been switched off. Wave after wave of memories hit me as each item was excavated, examined and set down. This was what I had been missing. How could I possibly have thought I could survive without them?

What on earth had I been thinking?

No matter!

We were reunited at last.

A tentative shuffling and a quiet, yet deliberate clearing of the throat broke into my bubble of contentment.

Beloved Husband was leaning against the door jam, the radio, now silent, in his hands. There was a carefully neutral expression on his face as he surveyed the room. (The football must be over. The storm certainly was.)

"So," he said cautiously, "it's starting again."

A statement.

Not a question.

I looked guiltily at the mess I had generated in the hall behind him and then at the pile of things on the table beside me.

"It does rather look as though it might be," I agreed.

I couldn't deny how happy the sight of my easel, brushes, pallet knives and sponges made me. Not to mention the way the sheer range of brightly coloured paints before me lifted my spirits.

My old friends were back!

Was that a hint of fear behind the carefully non-judgemental expression on Beloved Husband's face? Quite possibly!

Thinking back I can't really blame him. He was no doubt remembering what life was like when I painted before. Wet canvasses littering every surface in the house, my obsession with painting invading everything, the forgotten meals, the late nights and early mornings spent throwing colours at canvasses because little things like food and sleep just weren't as important as capturing a particular image in paint.

Could he be recalling the time he came home from work one day to find that a moment of inattention on my part had allowed our youngest offspring, dressed only in a nappy, to express his artistic side with an entire tube of Alizarin Crimson oil paint all over himself and our brand new conservatory?

Perhaps he is remembering the moment when we stood side by side staring in paralyzed horror at what we initially thought was the scene of a bloodbath (Alizarin Crimson really does resemble that most red of bodily fluids.) before we realised that the semi-naked two year old, writhing on the floor at our feet was not suffering a terrible death, but was in fact enjoying himself immensely.

It is sad to say that the split second of intense parental relief that he was unharmed was swiftly followed by our homeowners' instinctive urge to inflict bodily harm on the little vandal. This impulse was thankfully quickly superseded, primarily by Beloved Husband's compulsion to rescue the conservatory and secondly by my guilty need to extract the miniature criminal from the scene and clean him.

I rather think Beloved Husband got the easier job because at least the conservatory didn't wriggle around and protest vociferously at the liberal application of appropriate cleaning products.

Given our youngest child's total aversion to bath time on any given occasion, the extended period of cleaning time it took to remove all traces of crimson oil paint from every nook and cranny of his person was probably punishment enough.

For both of us!

Thank goodness the little ruffian's older sister was around to help hold him still. Wet two year olds are slippery little critters.

Then to add insult to injury I had to clean the bathroom and myself afterwards. Fortunately his sister was old enough to clean herself.

It was my own fault really, for taking my eyes off him. This particular child was exceptionally good at getting into mischief.

Thank heaven oil paint takes such a long time to dry.

An extended telephone call to the GP followed as we tried to decide whether the offender had actually consumed any paint and might therefore require some form of medical attention. The conclusion was that, as he appeared entirely unaltered from his customary destructive self (apart from an unusual degree of cleanliness), it would be kinder to spare the casualty department and the doctor politely suggested that we keep a close eye on him at home.

Beloved Husband was remarkably restrained under the circumstances and did not point out that I should have been doing that in the first place.

Accidental Damage

That particular event rather marked an important moment in my painting career as I locked the oil paints away and invested in water colours and acrylics, which are altogether less toxic and less permanent. I painted quite contentedly with these new materials until that terrible day when I turned my back on my art completely.

Now they were back!

All of them.

Watercolours, acrylics and oils, all jostling for space on the study table!

Beloved Husband could be forgiven for being somewhat concerned at such a development.

"I'll be careful," I said earnestly.

There was a moment of silence before he shook his head, rolled his eyes to the heavens and said with a wry smile "Of course you will!" He walked over and placed the radio carefully down on the windowsill switching it back on at a more moderate volume than before.

Then he turned to go, shoving the pile of discarded items back into the under-stairs cupboard and wedging the door closed as he went past.

Looking back at my old friends on the desk, I couldn't wait to get started. Within minutes there was a canvas clamped to the easel and my fingers itched to get hold of a paintbrush as I rummaged through tubes of colours.

Alice May

It crossed my mind to wonder how on earth I had survived without doing this for so long. Painting had always been my comfort, so perhaps now, with all my materials around me, I stood a chance of working out how to feel better about myself.

With absolutely no idea what I was going to paint I simply picked up a brush, selected a pot of paint at random and set to work.

2: Barbarian
Definition: a member of a primitive or uncivilised people.

The next morning, having fallen into bed incredibly late and then risen insanely early in order to continue painting, I was contentedly immersed in shades of sap green. I became aware of a rhythmic crunching sound coming from behind me. Gradually surfacing from a cocoon of colour, canvas and comforting brushstrokes I turned and focused on the figure looming in the doorway. Systematically spooning milk and cereal from a bowl into his face, my older son was observing me with interest.

He is the third in the series of small people that my Beloved Husband and I had created several years previously. At 16 he is getting surprisingly tall, which might have something to do with the fact that he is *always* eating.

Currently sporting pyjama bottoms and nothing else, he obviously hasn't stopped to get dressed before initiating his primary raid on the cereal cupboard this morning. I resisted the urge to tell him to go and put a top on and made a mental note to turn the heating down. It's mid-January for goodness sake! If people feel comfortable walking round in their scanties in the middle of winter then we obviously have the thermostat set far too high.

Now, it should be remembered that this son of ours is not someone who talks very much. This is potentially related to the fact that he is always mid-way through a snack. (I would like to believe that my numerous nags concerning not talking with your mouth full were inwardly digested, but I rather think not.) It's probably got more to do with the fact that I created two rather gobby older sisters for him before I got around to the job of manufacturing boys.

Don't misunderstand me, even though he is known affectionately to the family as Quiet, he can definitely talk. He just doesn't. Not very often, and when he does it's generally so brief you can easily miss it if you aren't concentrating, so I simply looked at him and waited patiently in case any utterances were imminently forthcoming.

He munched thoughtfully and then nodded slowly.

Then he chomped some more, while a kamikaze droplet of milk made its way down his chin and quivered momentarily before launching itself towards the floor.

Yet still there was no obviously impending comment. I got bored of waiting and raised an inquisitive eye at him, effectively inviting him to either speak or naff off. (Two could play at being uncommunicative.)

Getting the hint he finally swallowed and said, 'You're painting!'

Such a bright boy!! It's no wonder that Beloved Husband and I are so proud of him!

Usually, when Quiet finally does express himself I generally think it is worth listening to, as so much thought goes into it. Unlike most of the population he usually only speaks when he has something useful to say.

Still waters run deep and all that.

Accidental Damage

On this occasion, however, I realised that I might have to lower my expectations, so I nodded and turned back to my canvas.

"Good," he surprised me by continuing. I had thought I'd had my quota of words from him for the day.

"Really?" I enquired, deliberately not looking at him in case he stopped interacting altogether, "and why's that?"

This should be interesting.

Silence! I could almost hear him shrugging his shoulders — a favourite method of communication for most teenage boys.

He sighed heavily and I looked round meeting his eyes. They were sparkling with supressed humour and I could tell that he was calculating whether or not he would get away with his next statement.

I braced myself.

He tipped his head to one side and obviously decided to go for it.

"You're a lot less grumpy when you paint." He gave me a wicked grin and ambled off to find someone more entertaining to torment with his silent presence.

Cheeky beggar!

I returned to my soothing sap green canvas.

Grumpy, Hah! I'll show him grumpy!

Green, lovely green. Now what?

Purple? Deep, dark purple! Hmmmm. Yes purple will do nicely.

***

Sometime later I noticed a steaming hot cup of tea and a small plate piled high with chocolate chip cookies which had magically materialised on the table to my left. Could this be a peace offering to appease the painting spirits?

It's more likely to be my daughter's attempt to remind me that I have to eat. Logic is nearly 18 and is the second oldest in our tribe. As her nick-name suggests she is blessed with common sense, rationality and sound judgement. In short she is incredibly sensible, or might she only appear so when compared to her siblings? (I couldn't possibly comment.)

She is also the one of my off-spring that resembles me the most in looks. Poor child! In other words she is short and dark. I have no idea how her older sister got to be so tall or so naturally blonde, it must therefore be Beloved Husband's fault.

When faced with a situation she can't control Logic resorts to calories. I don't mean that she eats them (although she is perfectly capable of demolishing her own body weight in chocolate if she feels like it, I've seen her) I mean that if someone has a problem she can't fix for them then her solution is to produce food. A trait she has inherited from me.

Accidental Damage

Once I realised that cute little babies turned into uncivilised little savages, I accepted that I might have bitten off more than I could chew. Beloved Husband and I had foolishly outnumbered ourselves by initially having three of the little monsters in fairly quick succession, so we set about working out how to contain the situation, swiftly establishing the fact that feeding them on a regular basis kept them relatively content and made them less likely to tear the place and each other (not to mention us) apart.

Having instigated a degree of control over the first three, Beloved Husband and I, lulled into a false sense of security, then decided to have number four a few years later. We thought that it really couldn't have been that bad before.

Then we remembered.

Four was definitely our limit. Luckily a regular input of food tamed this last arrival as well. To a point anyway!

Thus over the years whenever one of my small hooligans has approached me with an issue, my first act is to open the biscuit tin, place it between them and me and then stand well back.

***

Over the years a degree of civilisation has been established within our little band. In fact a peace treaty, successfully negotiated between the grown-ups and the Barbarians, is currently flourishing.

This agreement involves basic things such as the production of relatively adequate grades at school, not swearing in front of grandparents and the use of rudimentary table manners in exchange for an unlimited supply of food (including fruit and vegetables), donations of cash on occasion and lifts to their mates' houses when needed. After all we do live in the middle of nowhere.

On the whole a happy medium has been achieved and the Barbarians cannot in truth be referred to as Barbarians any longer. (But that's not going to stop me. Who said life was fair?)

***

Anyway where was I? Oh yes I was drinking my tea in the study and chomping contentedly away on cookies. I studied the large canvas before me with a degree of bemused surprise. It was now sporting a selection of gigantic bluebells. Rather different from my old style, a bit outlandish maybe, but definitely quite relaxed and free.

While I looked at it I was surprised to experience an emotion that I struggled to identify. It was so long since I had felt anything like it, but could I possibly be relaxing just a little bit? I wasn't really sure, but thought I'd better paint a bit more and find out. (Any excuse!)

Now that I was starting to feel a bit better about myself I decided that it was high time I examined the events of two and a half years ago to try and work out at exactly what point the old 'me' had become broken and why.

Concluding that I rather liked the bluebells, I leaned in to sign my name at the bottom, before reaching for a fresh blank canvas and casting my mind back.

3: <u>Cob</u>

Definition: an ancient construction material used for building since prehistoric times. Traditionally, English cob consists of clay-based subsoil mixed with sand, straw and water and trampled by oxen.

Two and a half years previously....

When you buy old properties you can expect them to be a teeny bit troublesome.

Our house was no exception. Young and naïve as we might have been when we bought it, we weren't completely daft. We could see that work was required yet we could also see that the rather random conglomeration of structures that encompassed the sweet old cottage, presented us with the opportunity to build an idyllic life in the countryside for our growing band of marauding Barbarians.

There were plenty of bedrooms upstairs and a huge garden for prowling around, surrounded by fields and streams to explore. Loads of fresh air so the asthmatics would thrive, plus it was miles away from the hustle and bustle of main roads and big cities.

In effect, by living here, we could be said to be protecting both the Barbarians and society, at the same time.

The house consisted of a motley selection of extensions of indeterminate age around a central cob cottage. The original structure had been present on the site for at least 350 years, but had been altered to a sufficiently unrecognisable degree that the local planners were not skipping round it trying to put it on one of their lists of historical significance.

This was a good thing as it meant that we would be able to get planning permission to make some alterations. Nevertheless we still had National Park (NP), Area of Outstanding Natural Beauty (AONB), Site of Special Scientific Interest (SSSI) and River Corridor designations to contend with so no changes were going to be particularly straight forward. (We wouldn't want straight forward would we, that would make life far too boring wouldn't it?)

Over the next ten years we slowly spruced up bits of the cottage as our finances allowed, but the original section remained much as we had found it. Lovely thick, solid walls, warm in winter and cool in summer. There was a charmingly rickety staircase that would never pass building regulations these days and a huge open fireplace with old foot and hand holds leading up the inside of the vast chimney stack. (No we never sent any of the Barbarians up it, even though it was very tempting to save on the chimney sweep bills!) The whole thing was topped off with a very pretty thatched roof.

We had been assured by the detailed structural survey that it was all completely sound and thus no concerns were raised. The general consensus from all consulted was that it had stood for 350 years already it would stand for 350 more.

So you can understand my total incomprehension as I stood on the driveway one July day and watched as two massive jagged cracks tore their way up the walls of my home from ground level right up to pretty thatched roof and a section of cob started to move very slowly away from the rest of the house.

Accidental Damage

"How peculiar!" I remember thinking, as my Friendly Local Builder and his mate, who had fortuitously popped by at that exact moment to pick up some previously forgotten equipment, frantically swung into action.

An amazing co-incidence it is true, but there they were, builders, just when I needed them the most. How often does that happen? Perhaps someone was smiling on me from on high that day, despite all evidence to the contrary.

Experienced in construction work as these builders were, they were able to size up what was going on in lightening quick time. So while I was staring in incomprehension, my companions were hastily trying to erect some props that they happened to have in the back of their truck, in order to prevent the wall collapsing completely.

Standing rooted to the spot I could not believe my eyes. This couldn't possibly be happening!

Yet it clearly was. That second 350 years was rather demonstrably off the cards now. In fact the house looked as though it had got rather tired and had a little sit down. I didn't really blame it. I was feeling rather faint myself.

My mobile warbled and I answered it on automatic pilot.

"You alright?" chirped my blissfully unaware Beloved Husband.

"We have a slight problem," I croaked out.

***

Alice May

Twenty minutes later, Beloved Husband and I were both standing on the drive looking at the damage to our home in total silence. Words cannot begin to describe how dumbfounded we were.

I do remember thinking irrelevantly that at least it was rather a nice day. Blue sky, sunshine, tweeting birds, you know the kind I mean. Always looking for a silver lining, that's me, or at least it was. It probably would have been worse if it had been raining, but let's face it, things were pretty bad already.

Friendly Local Builder came over to us dusting off his hands and said, "OK, it's stable for now, but it's going to need a bit of work." A well-meant understatement, I think. Just like when the nurse says, "You won't feel a thing."

"I take it there's no-one inside?" he continued.

Oh damn! Was there? (No you're right I said something much worse than that but I am not admitting to it in print.)

The Barbarian Horde! Frantic mental mechanics ensued.

Phew panic over.

"It's OK," I stammered after a moment of carefully cataloguing the probable whereabouts of our offspring. "The kids are all at school, and the cat is asleep in the back garden."

"There's lucky then, could have been worse," he said cheerfully.

Accidental Damage

Beloved Husband and I looked at him in complete astonishment. Could there possibly be something lucky about this? Maybe he was right, after all no one was actually dead, except possibly the cottage. It all rather depended on your perspective I supposed.

"Best ring your house insurance then," he prompted helpfully.

We nodded, that did seem like the only thing to do under the circumstances.

***

A surprisingly short while later Beloved Husband had achieved a degree of communication with the house insurance company.

With my hands wrapped around a warm cup of tea, (we're British, what else were we going to do in a crisis?) I listened as he calmly agreed with the sweet young thing on the end of the line that it really was highly inconsiderate of us to allow the house to fall down on a Friday afternoon. However, after he had politely insisted that yes the situation was fairly critical and no it really couldn't wait until Monday, arrangements were eventually made for a structural engineer to visit the property to assess the situation later that evening.

Fingers crossed there was something of the house left standing for him to assess when he got here.

There had been rather a lot of haphazard development at the property over the course of its 350 year existence. The most useful addition at this present time was a fairly large, relatively modern, single storey extension at the rear of the original two storey cob section.

This was a very useful family room designed around a kitchen with a lounge-style seating area by an open fire to one side. The room then morphed into a conservatory / dining area towards the garden. There was also a door that led to a tiny ground floor bathroom with a miniscule utility area. Fortunately this part of the house could all safely be accessed via the conservatory doors by the back patio without risking our necks going near the worryingly, wobbly walls at the front.

As a result we were able to corral the Barbarian Horde, on their return from various educational establishments, at the back of the house with sufficient edible supplies, a selection of electronic entertainment equipment and a stern lecture about venturing no further than the bathroom and back on pain of death. Literally!

We bravely decided to survey the internal damage. On reflection this was probably a rather foolish idea, but I never have claimed to be terribly intelligent.

It was a very surreal experience. The cracks had widened considerably in a very short space of time, allowing loads more daylight to penetrate the small cottage rooms than we usually got from the tiny old windows. Unfortunately this additional lighting allowed us to see quite clearly the substantial internal damage that had resulted.

Friendly Local Builder had stuck around, not only for the entertainment value that we were offering, but also from a

Accidental Damage

genuine desire to help out. He muttered something about needing some more support and disappeared back outside to his truck. He returned shortly with a couple of metal props and a stack of three yellow hard hats. Beloved Husband and I accepted the hats in wordless disbelief and rammed them on our heads obediently before turning towards the stairs.

It was at this point that we began to get an inkling of quite how big a problem we now had. The previously charming, yet slightly rickety staircase was no longer charming and was significantly more rickety. In fact we would be hard put to describe it as a staircase at all. It had been built into the corner of the cob cottage where the slightly smaller of the two massive cracks now ran right up the stairwell towards the roof. (Not an interior design feature I would recommend.)

As Friendly Local Builder did something useful with his props downstairs, we ventured cautiously and no doubt imprudently up what remained of the staircase. I challenge anyone to make sound decisions under similar circumstances.

The damage to the upstairs was comparable to that downstairs, if not significantly worse. Plaster was still falling from the walls in huge chunks leaving thick dust swirling. Early evening sunlight poured in through a significant gap between the wall and the roof at one end, highlighting a scene of utter devastation.

Bedtime was obviously going to be a bit of an issue.

4: Insurance

Definition: a written agreement by which a company provides a guarantee of compensation for loss, damage, illness, or death in exchange for payment of a premium

Having finished our rather terrifying inspection of the first floor of our cottage, we heard the crunch of tyres on the driveway. It was clearly audible through the gap in the wall and peering out we could see a four by four pulling up. Carefully picking our way back down what had previously been the stairs we went to greet the new arrival.

A tall, rumpled and rather tired looking gentleman wearing an Aran jumper, corduroy trousers and walking boots, was standing on the drive, an air of complete exhaustion emanating from every pore and a black Labrador sitting obediently at his feet. It had no doubt been a long day for him, if not a long week and we were unbelievably grateful that he had added this one last site visit to his list.

He politely identified himself as the structural engineer from the house insurance company and shook hands with us before grabbing a clipboard and hard hat from his car.

He took his time examining the outside of the house, taking photos, walking up and down, examining the cracks closely and scribbling notes with the dog hard on his heels. Then to my surprise, he stepped through the larger of the cracks and straight into the cottage.

Beloved Husband and I looked at each other in silence.

Accidental Damage

In a matter of hours the cracks in the side of our house could no longer be described as 'cracks'. They were now such significantly large chasms that a grown man could walk through them.

With his dog!

In the general scheme of things I would usually expect a visitor to ask if it is ok before bringing their dog onto (and into) my property, but having never had a house with a yawning crater in the wall before I didn't know if the accepted etiquette was different so I decided to let it slide and simply followed them in.

Such a surreal feeling walking through the wall! What a shame we didn't find ourselves on a magical platform heading for our first term at a school for wizards when we emerged on the other side. Perhaps we should have taken more of a run up.

Structural Engineer Man then proceeded to crawl (quite literally in the case of the stairs, the first floor bedrooms and the loft) all over the interior of the cob section of the cottage making copious notes. He made several rather unfathomable comments aloud which Friendly Local Builder appeared to comprehend. Beloved Husband and I got the impression that these remarks concerned additional propping materials necessary in order to prevent any further slippage and so we eagerly agreed when Friendly Local Builder asked if we would like him to arrange it all. Obviously pleased to have something practical to do he beetled off to hire and install the necessary paraphernalia.

Eventually Structural Engineer Man ground to a halt and rumbled that he now had sufficient measurements recorded to make an initial report but that he had rather a lot of questions he needed to ask us as well. In view of the instability of the property he suggested that we retreat to a safer location at the back of the house.

"Of course I am not really an expert in these old buildings," he said ominously. "Nevertheless I can confirm that your cob is in serious trouble."

I could hear Beloved Husband making a concerted effort to bite his tongue and no wonder. We had spent a small fortune on house insurance over the years with a company that is supposed to know that this is an old building and then when we actually need them, they send us someone who is 'not an expert in old buildings'.

Great! It's taken him two hours to conclude that we are in trouble. We already knew that!

I took a deep, calming breath.

"I must strongly recommend to you that no one should access this part of your home," he continued. "You really should ensure you keep your dog out of here too."

"That's Ok" I reassured him. "We don't have a dog."

He gave me a very odd look at that point and then regarded the canine between us on the floor. The Labrador was looking up at us, tongue hanging out, panting cheerfully.

Accidental Damage

"It's Ok," I continued hoping I hadn't offended him. Whether he was an old buildings expert or not we really needed a helpful report from him. "We really don't mind that you brought your dog in with you. We do like dogs," I insisted. "We just don't own one."

He raised a quizzical eyebrow at me before looking down again and saying emphatically, "THAT is not my dog."

"Ah!"

I didn't really know what to say then and Beloved Husband was not much help either, having apparently lost the ability to speak entirely. (Between you and me not a bad thing just at that point.)

All three of us stood and looked at the dog for a moment before we heard a sharp whistle from the road outside and the dog shot off through the hole in the wall and disappeared.

"Shall I make us a nice cup of tea?" I suggested brightly, changing the subject.

5: Chaos

Definition: a collection of elements without organisation or connection.

Back to the future (I am not referring to the film!).....

Having completed a rather hectic school run (yes we were late as usual) the next day, followed by a hasty supermarket trip to restock the cupboards with relatively healthy provisions after a weekend of plundering by my starving teenage savages, I was energetically engaged in priming another canvas.

The breakfast show was emanating from my battered old radio. It was still sat on the windowsill where Beloved Husband had left it, and had since been joined, at some point, by the cat. Extremely elderly and looking decidedly scruffy these days, (a bit like the radio) the aforementioned feline was enjoying the January sunshine whilst politely ignoring me.

Having carefully hidden my feelings about what had happened for so long, I was amazed at how quickly I was changing my mind. The more I thought about it, the more I wanted to get these damaging emotions out so that I didn't have to waste energy trying to suppress them anymore. While I didn't yet actually want to talk to anyone about it, transferring my emotions onto the canvas before me was definitely helping.

Luckily I had found several large, abandoned, blank canvases stuffed behind the freezer in the garage. (No, I don't know how they got there.) I reasoned that as they weren't costing me anything I would just let my re-discovered creative spirit wander across them and see what resulted.

So the insistent 'bing-boing' of an unexpected Skype call interrupted some fairly intense concentration on my part.

Reluctantly I put my brush down, muted the radio and flicked the I-pad open to accept the call, absentmindedly taking an enormous bite from the piece of chocolate fudge cake that had materialised on my desk next to a huge cup of tea. I wondered where on earth they had come from and concluded that it must be a Tuesday. Logic gets the day off college on a Tuesday and therefore was capable of making tea and cake appear out of the blue.

How had I not noticed that she wasn't in the car when I did the school run? Was the need to paint fogging my brain quite that much already? (Note to self: I really must try to pay more attention!)

"Hello Oldest Offspring!" I said cheerfully to the I-pad screen.

No, I am not psychic! Chaos is the only person on the planet who ever Skypes me. Her nickname is appropriate for one who lives her life in fast forward. Believe me you never quite know what she is going to do next!

Skyping is a technological advancement that I had studiously avoided until one of my Barbarians actually left home for university and I was forced to embrace the world of modern communication systems in order to reassure myself that she was OK.

Well wouldn't you be curious if you had single-handedly let Chaos loose in the big wide world?

"Hi mum. How are you?" she asked sunnily, and then immediately froze in an unflattering pose that meant I could see right up her nostrils. Usually the internet here is very good but occasionally there are minor blips that make Skype calls more entertaining.

Internet aside, there were a number of things that Beloved Husband and I should have considered before we naively bought a ramshackle property in such a remote area. Luxuries like mains drainage, a gas supply, reliable telephone and electricity connections, not to mention pavements, street lighting and public transport should have been given at least a passing consideration, but we were young and foolish. (We're still foolish, but sadly not so young anymore.)

Nevertheless the very rare drop out of the internet signal has had its uses in the ever constant parental battle against the terrible teens' insistence on living their lives entirely through social media.

"Oh dear!" I have been known to cry on occasion, having accidentally (on purpose) switched the internet off. "The internet is down! What a shame! Never mind, it's dinner time, let's all come to the table. Maybe the signal will be back up by the time we've finished eating."

This approach does, however, require the co-operation of Beloved Husband, who, if not pre-warned that this is an intentional tactic, has been known to race through the kitchen flicking the appropriate switch to re-establish connection and then claiming loudly to have 'fixed it'. What follows are rapturous cries of delighted hero-worship from the Barbarian Horde. Then both he and they all immediately return to the act of frying their brains through electronic media whilst simultaneously developing deep vein thromboses.

The lovingly prepared, healthy dinner goes cold and dry on the table and Beloved Husband (eventually) wonders why I am not talking to him.

But I digress….

"I am good," I responded when her image started to move again indicating that we had an active connection once more. "You?"

"Yeah! Good," she says.

There followed a silence that I eventually broke. "Go on then Chaos, what are you calling me for so early on a Tuesday morning? I know you don't have lectures until twelve so it must be important for you to be awake this early. Spill!"

"I heard on the grapevine that you are painting again."

"And?"

"Well I was just interested…..Can I see?"

I turned the I-pad around so she could see the barmy bluebells propped up in the corner.

"Wow! That's a bit different from your usual style. It's true then."

"So it would appear," I confirmed dryly. It's rather gratifying to realise that, contrary to appearance, the Barbarian Horde do actually pay attention to what's going on in this house, and also choose to communicate with each other voluntarily. That includes those who no longer live here permanently any more.

Like most mothers I could be forgiven for thinking that no one would actually notice if I were to disappear off the face of the planet, until the supply of food and clean clothes ran out of course.

"That's good," she continued. (She doesn't mean my bluebells, but I don't take it personally.)

"Yeah, I know. Your brother already gave me the 'you'll be less grumpy if you're painting' line, thank you very much."

"Ha!" She let out a delighted squeal. "He never did? Is he still breathing?"

"I was remarkably restrained," I agreed, mentally congratulating myself on my older son's continued existence on the planet (for now).

"There you go then, that proves his point," she said triumphantly and paused before continuing in a more serious tone, "I always wondered why you stopped... you loved it so much....can I ask .....was it me?"

There was a pause while I looked at her blankly. 'Typical teen', one might be forgiven for thinking. Obviously the world does revolve around them. However in this case I got the impression that there was a bit more to it than that.

"What do you mean?" I asked.

"You stopped painting nearly three years ago, around about the time that I......" she tailed off rather sheepishly.

The penny dropped, "Oh!" I said, seeing where she was going with this. "No. Don't worry it wasn't you."

"Are you sure?"

"Yes, I promise."

"Really? Because I .."

"Chaos," I broke in forcefully, "I promise you that your little flirtation with the Grim Reaper did not make me stop painting. OK? It was all that other stuff that came afterwards, and that was nothing to do with you."

"OK." She smiled. "Well I am glad you have started again and I rather like the bluebells. They're big and a bit bonkers but they're still kinda cute. Anyway, gotta go, lectures and all that. Love ya."

With that typically casual goodbye she was gone.

Obviously now that she'd been absolved of any responsibility for the cessation of my painting career she was not really that interested in the real reason why I had stopped.

I was though. At the time it had seemed like the only option.

Alice May

Practical.

Necessary.

In fact, essential.

I am not sure I had ever really acknowledged it even to myself. It had been an immediate, unconsidered knee jerk reaction to circumstance and all stopped thereafter.

Now that I was painting again it seemed unbelievable that I could ever have considered stopping. I looked at my bluebells again thoughtfully. They were not bonkers. Admittedly the style was far more casual than anything I had painted before but I liked them. Nevertheless I pondered if I would ever paint like I had before, precise, meticulous, detailed pieces of work.

Probably not was the answer. I was a completely different person now. I'd been emotionally bashed and broken, but perhaps I could now hear a little voice calling quietly from way down deep inside me, "I am still here!"

In a small way Chaos was correct in that her little dalliance with death a few years previously had inevitably had a massive impact on us all. This was about six months before the house fell down. (Yes, I know, it probably wasn't the luckiest of years for us!) She went from being 100% healthy and never ill a day in her life, to 99.9% extremely not very well at all.

Overnight.

Accidental Damage

I won't go into details, mainly because other people's health issues are always so boring. (Anyway she'd totally kill me and, more importantly, I might need to blackmail her with the information at some point in the future. I am not giving away that particular advantage here.) Suffice to say that she suddenly required emergency surgery. We did our bit and transported her to hospital. We've seen Casualty, we know the drill! Once there we waited, confident that the good old NHS would roll in and save the day.

Only they nearly couldn't as the contrary little madam developed unexpected complications.

It's a soap opera every minute in this family.

A little bit of emergency surgery couldn't possibly go smoothly for us now could it?

Beloved Husband and I were left to ferment in her allocated hospital bay on the paediatric ward. We'd seen the bed, with her in it, being wheeled off to theatre. The curtains were drawn round where the bed used to be and we sat inside them on orange plastic chairs (the sort that can be wiped down if you have an unfortunate accident) looking at the big empty bed-sized space and we waited.

And waited.

And waited some more.

Eventually, totally stressed, (and also desperate for the loo as we hadn't dared go anywhere in-case we missed someone arriving with news, so no wonder they have wipe-down chairs) we were relieved to see the Eminent Surgeon whisk through the curtains with several members of his team and start to talk to us.

I noted with concern that he was looking alarmingly pale, sweaty and exhausted before I tuned into what he was actually saying. I struggled to get my confused brain around the words he was using. There were quite a lot of references to 'unfortunate ruptures'...... 'internal bleeding'.... 'difficulties suturing'....'loss of several pints' etc.... before he finished with "but she's going to be OK now."

Phew! Honestly, I ask you, could he not have started the conversation with that last bit?

It all happened so fast that we didn't really realise that the whole event had been touch and go until it was all over. I probably could have gone into a flat spin about it but there wasn't really time to have a nervous breakdown just then.

There followed an extensive period of recovery, more surgical procedures and months of rehabilitation, physiotherapy etc, which meant that I was constantly driving her to follow-up appointments and therapy sessions as well as trying to juggle the other Barbarians' schedules.

Oh! Not to forget going to work and doing my job too. There seriously was no time for anything else. So from a practical point of view it did essentially physically stop me painting. But it wasn't what stopped me actually wanting to paint.

The house falling down wasn't the reason either. Nothing is ever that simple. (Beloved Husband would be the first to assure you that I am a very complicated individual.) The event that stopped me actually wanting to paint came later and it is that which came so close to destroying me completely.

PART 2

That which does not kill us makes us stronger.

Friedrich Nietzsche

6: <u>Serenity</u>

Definition: The state of being trouble free, peaceful and calm.

Present day still....

Contentment comes in many forms. In my case I had always had the ability to become so absorbed in laying down colours on canvas that the troubles of the world would simply fade away. Problems became non-existent and my spirits were lifted. Mucking about, elbow deep in paint, had always enabled me to sort things out in my head, as if by inspiring the imaginative part of my brain through painting I was able to understand other areas of my life more effectively. It gave me control and peace simultaneously, regardless of how successful (or not) I felt the final piece of work was.

Whilst contemplating Chaos' illness and recovery, and also the initial collapse of our house a few months later, I had subconsciously and systematically filled a second canvas with colour. This time when I finally surfaced from my thoughts I saw a dark series of rather demented and dishevelled-looking daisies staring back at me.

No doubt about it, psychologically challenged flora was my new theme.

Nevertheless I was beginning to delve tentatively deeper into the question of why I had stopped painting. I had always refused to let my mind wander into that murky territory. Perhaps I was afraid of what I would find. Time to finish that fudge cake perhaps! Now where did I put it?

Accidental Damage

I had deliberately shut my painting down two and a half years ago, immediately, completely and absolutely. A realisation so terrible had dawned, one that I couldn't control or fix.

My fundamental belief that everything would be alright if you just did your best was whipped away from me like a rug being literally pulled from beneath my feet. Everything I held dear was threatened. Beloved Husband, the adored Barbarian Horde and our cosy protected home life were all in jeopardy, and I had not been able prevent it. In fact I had potentially contributed to events, inadvertently making the consequences far worse.

In response had I amputated an essential part of myself as a punishment? No one had made me do it. The decision was entirely mine, a calculatingly measured action at a time when I had so little power over anything else that was happening.

The price I had paid personally as a result of that whole event had been so very far reaching. Even now, over two years on, I was still damaged. I found it hard to trust myself to make the right decisions.

To put it bluntly, because of what had happened, I was living in fear.

Nonetheless, the world continues to turn, and we must move forward. I can't stand that ghastly American term 'closure'. This is not about 'closure' it's about survival.

Eventually we must face those things that scare us. We need to confront them head on, because only then can we stand a chance of defeating them so that they can't dominate the rest of our lives.

Setting the disconcerting daisy canvas to one side I reached for a blank one. I wondered if I was strong enough to revisit the source of my deepest pain.

There was only one way to find out.

7: <u>Expert</u>

Definition: A person who has gained a high degree of skill in or knowledge of a particular specialist subject

Returning to the somewhat wobbly cottage in the past...

While I put the kettle on Structural Engineer Man settled himself into a chair at the kitchen table for what looked like it might be a relatively lengthy stay.

He dumped his clipboard down and suddenly took off his jumper in that rather incredible way that I have only ever seen men do. He reached behind his head to the middle of his back, grabbed a handful of material and yanked it up and over. I watched this manoeuvre in fascinated bemusement, wondering how he managed it without dislocating something essential.

It's probably the same for fellas when they see a woman remove her bra (let me finish!) *without* taking off her top first. They just can't work out how we do that can they? We unclip, wriggle about a bit and suddenly out the bra pops from a sleeve. Not that I go around doing that in public you understand.

His head eventually reappeared from the folds of fabric and all his floppy, blond hair stood on end with the static, forming a crackly, golden halo. I placed a large mug of caffeine and a sugar bowl on the table before him while he hurriedly tried to make his hair behave in a more acceptable and professional manner.

Meanwhile, Beloved Husband had recovered the power of speech and was making a hasty phone call.

As he had left work in a hurry earlier that day muttering that his house might be falling down, a helpful colleague had jokingly said that he had an eight man tent if we needed it. This phone call was to ascertain how serious Helpful Colleague actually was with regard to the lending of the tent as it was now patently obvious that we had nowhere to sleep. It was getting late and there was no sign of a Helpful House Insurance Man to whisk us off to a comfortable hotel. Wouldn't that be nice?

To be totally fair, if a Helpful House Insurance Man was to have appeared at that point, he would have had quite a job to whisk us off to a hotel without having to build one first.

It was July and the height of the summer silly-season in the nearby coastal town was upon us. By that I mean that the school holidays were just beginning and every hotel, travel lodge, caravan park and bed and breakfast within a thirty mile radius would have been booked solid months in advance. Even were a few cancellations available there's just no way that a Helpful House Insurance Man would have been able to find accommodation for six of us together in one location.

Probably just as well he didn't exist.

It would have been a shame to raise our hopes.

As it happens Helpful Colleague kindly dropped round the tent. The Barbarian Horde pounced on this new form of entertainment and set about erecting it in the garden before the light faded.

While that was going on Beloved Husband and I did our best to answer all the questions that Structural Engineer Man asked us. He carefully noted all our answers down on his clipboard and eventually took himself off, telling us that he would file his report as soon as possible and that we would shortly hear from the Insurance Company with regard to our claim.

Both statements, though no doubt well intentioned, turned out to be somewhat divorced from the truth.

When his report finally did materialise nearly three weeks later it blamed the wall collapse on the fact that the roof was too heavy.

I have to confess that I had real trouble believing that this was the cause of the damage.

One could point out at this juncture that the roof had been in place for many, many years and logic would surely dictate that there would have been an issue with the wall long before now if it had genuinely been too heavy.

But what do I know? I am not an old buildings expert either.

Interestingly, though, the roof was actually still in place, having not moved an inch in spite of a significant part of two walls giving way. Probably not 'too heavy' then, as Genuine Old Building Expert was later to confirm in his subsequent report.

However, I am rushing ahead, we haven't met Genuine Old Building Expert yet, and we won't for quite a while.

Unfortunately.

In the meantime we had more delights to come from the House Insurance Team, including the arrival of Loss Adjuster Number 1.

But not for a while.

We had several days to survive first before he showed up.

Several days during which Beloved Husband and I started systematically stripping the cob section of the cottage of all important articles. Each trip up the stairs involved keeping a careful eye on the cracks to see if they were still moving before grabbing and bolting with whatever essential items we could get our hands on.

Mattresses, clothes, school work (Chaos, at 17, was about to embark on her second A level year and Logic, at 16, was soon to start AS levels, not to mention Quiet's GCSE courses, so yes school work did count as essential.) bedding, sports kit, make up (very necessary for teenage girls apparently) and other bedroom paraphernalia, were all dragged downstairs one bit at a time and deposited in jumbled heaps on the covered patio at the back of the house.

Then we got to work dismantling furniture and bringing down bed frames, wardrobes, desks, anything we could get access to really and hauling them down a piece at a time to dump in piles in the garage, while trying to keep all the relevant screws and bolts together in small sandwich bags taped to each item.

This furniture dismantling operation was the scariest bit so far, as it involved staying put upstairs for fairly long periods of time during which the creaking and settling of the 'possibly' (i.e. definitely) still moving house happened loudly around us.

We weren't daft, (well apart from the bit where we repeatedly entered an unstable building that we had been warned to stay out of) we could see that the cottage was not going to be habitable for quite a long period and may in fact need to come down entirely. Regardless of what the house insurance did or did not do, we had to find a way to establish a reasonably acceptable, temporary (we hoped) existence.

****

Friendly Local Builder popped back several times over the weekend, having managed to procure yet more propping equipment. He merrily installed lots more metal scaffolding poles, wooden wedges and other strengthening apparatus.

"Better safe than sorry," he said cheerfully as we all consumed yet more tea whilst watching the walls for any signs of further movement.

I am not joking!

When you've seen them move once you can't help but keep watching in case they do it again, it's somewhat ominously addictive.

Alice May

Our poor little home looked like it had had a major stroke. It's formerly pretty, little, cottagey face sagged alarmingly all down one side with an upstairs window hanging at a wonky angle and the previously central porch roof tipping over rather drunkenly. After so many years of chocolate-box beauty she now looked sick, old and so very tired that it made my heart ache with despair.

Inevitably our Friendly Local Builder was keen to be invited to quote for whatever work might be necessary to fix the current situation but we were at the mercy of the insurance company procedure before we could make any such decisions. Off the record, though, we did discuss vague potential building options and he gave us some very scary costings.

It basically boiled down to the fact that we were possibly looking at a bill of well over £200,000, if not much, much more.

Beloved Husband had to take himself off for an extended lie down.

I couldn't really blame him.

Friendly Local Builder eventually exited stage left, issuing the helpful suggestion that if we were determined to risk our necks by repeatedly entering the unstable structure, which he wouldn't advise, it would be a good idea to empty the loft while we were at it.

Righto!

Accidental Damage

Thus I found myself up a ladder explaining the disastrous situation to the spiders squatting in the loft when Beloved Husband eventually felt up to re-joining the party. Thankfully he then bravely took over all loft jurisdiction and spider taming duties. My hero! I really hate lofts.

We made a pact between us that we should only be present in the unstable section of the house one at a time. This decision was based on the general consensus that it would be preferable for the Barbarian Horde not to lose both parents should the house fall completely.

Admittedly not very happy logic, but we were trying to be relatively sensible. Obviously the Barbarian Horde were banned from the wobbly bit entirely, but keen to be useful they formed a line along which to pass items through the rest of the house and out onto the patio. The piles of stuff were getting very large and extremely random now, spilling some significant distance out onto the garden. Fortunately the weather was reasonably fine, but we did try to keep the most fragile items under cover and dragged large sheets of polythene, unearthed from the garage, over all the rest in case it rained before we could sort and distribute items to as yet undisclosed and unidentified storage locations.

It is a very sobering thing to see your entire home contents laid out across your garden. It definitely made us want to reach for neat alcohol, and lots of it. However we restricted ourselves to one small beer each that evening. We potentially had £200,000 to find now, so there would sadly be no spare money for sufficiently strong spirits to anaesthetise us. Current supplies were going to have to be rationed carefully.

Alice May

Beloved Husband and I eventually stopped sorting things and sat on a pile of boxes in the conservatory, exhausted, having ensured that all the Barbarians were as cosily wrapped up in the tent as possible. He still wasn't saying very much at all. Periodically he would mutter "£200,000" and shake his head in disbelief, rocking backwards and forwards disturbingly, but nothing else terribly coherent was forthcoming.

After a very long heavy silence I remember saying, "if you are thinking of driving to Beachy Head and jumping off, can I come too?"

You could hear a pin drop the room was so quiet.

"Hmmmm." He said vaguely.

There was a deathly silence.

"Of course," I eventually continued thoughtfully, "that probably wouldn't be very fair to the Barbarian Horde would it?"

More pins dropping.

"Hmmmm."

"No, you're right," (me again,) "and I suppose that, house insurance claim issue aside, we can guarantee that the life insurance would *definitely* not pay out if we do jump off."

Accidental Damage

A whole tin of pins went crashing to the floor.

"Hmmmmmmmmmm."

"So, probably best not eh?"

"Hmmmmmmmmmmmmmmmmmmmmmmm."

"Yeah," I agreed, "You're right!"

8: <u>Soon</u>

Definition: taking place within a short period of time, promptly or speedily.

Still in the past...

The next day was a Monday. Wonderful!

If you think the normal school run on a Monday is entertaining you should try doing it from a tent in your back garden. It is vastly more diverting.

Especially, when that tent is surrounded by the dismantled and jumbled up contents of your entire home! Added to that we were down to one extremely small bathroom for six of us and we all had to get ready for work and school in a very short space of time.

Usually the first hour of our weekday mornings consists of a tightly scheduled bathroom rota system worked out carefully to enable all six of us to utilise one of two showers, get dressed, clean teeth etc. Then a short period of time follows for breakfast, the finding of lost shoes, ties, bags, homework and miscellaneous other items before we eventually tumble into the car with at least almost everything we need for the day. Then finally setting off for school and work with something resembling a packed lunch and a vague hope of arriving in time.

Slightly more complicated from a tent in the middle of a disaster site.

Accidental Damage

Nevertheless we managed it and I finally arrived at work only mildly more late than usual and sat with a hot cup of tea looking numbly at the pile of paperwork awaiting my attention.

"Lucky me!" I thought and then jumped as my mobile sprang into life.

A brief conversation ensued, after which I rattled off a quick text to Beloved Husband as follows: 'Loss adjuster on way to our house now, ETA 15 minutes, meet me if you can'. Leaving my computer on and some papers strategically placed so as to appear as if I were in the middle of something but had been called away on legitimate office business, I swiftly exited the building, hoping no one would notice I was moving in entirely the wrong direction for that time of the morning. Then I drove hell for leather for home. (Or should that now be tent? It hasn't quite got the same ring to it!)

Beloved Husband and I arrived home simultaneously and waited in suspended animation for Loss Adjuster Number 1 to turn up.

Forty minutes later a car squealed around the corner and onto the driveway scattering pea shingle in a multitude of directions. Normally that really bugs Beloved Husband. (I only ever do it as a subversive form of revenge when he's really winding me up.)

The driver, a short, rotund gentleman with thinning hair worn in an ambitious comb over, opened the car door forcefully and stepped out onto one leg, leaving the other foot dangling in the foot well. He was obviously not planning to stick around very long.

After a cursory glance at the crumbly cottage walls he nodded at us in acknowledgement.

"Yes, well," he said rapidly, "all very unfortunate of course. I'll be in touch soon to let you know if you're covered."

With that he flung his capacious backside down into the driving seat, slammed the door and reversed off the driveway at speed.

Obviously a very busy man!

Not quite what the TV ad had implied was standard behaviour for the house insurance company personnel in a crisis scenario.

Hey ho! Let's not get too hung up on semantics.

After a several moments of stunned silence I ventured to speak. "That was…..um……promising….!?!"

"Hmm!" replied Beloved Husband, nodding slowly before patting my arm gently, then heading back to his car and driving away - hopefully back to work and not towards Beachy Head.

I didn't have the energy to find out which so started my car engine and set off for my own office.

****

Accidental Damage

It quickly became patently obvious to me that Loss Adjuster Number 1 and I held wildly different definitions of what "I'll be in touch soon," actually meant, as the days drifted into a week.

Then longer.

In the interests of being fair, it probably is a relatively short period of time if one is living in a nice, warm, dry home rather than camping out in ruins.

Normally I would have been on the phone to him within 48 hours, and again every hour after that until I got a response, if I hadn't had Beloved Husband (in surprisingly reasonable mode) saying patiently, "Give the poor chap a chance, he probably hasn't even received Structural Engineer Man's report yet."

Now you might think that Beloved Husband is the epitome of calm, rationality but I know better. He had stuck his head quite firmly in the sand. He was completely convinced that the House Insurance had no intention of helping us and he simply couldn't cope with having that fact confirmed, because then we'd have to come up with a plan of action on our own. He knew that neither of us had a clue what that plan might be.

Yes he is occasionally a glass-half-empty kind of guy, but not always and under the circumstances, can you blame him?

I couldn't.

He is usually the person I turn to for help fixing problems when I can't work them out for myself. He has a real skill for finding solutions and often comes up with some remarkably ingenious ways to sort things out.

Only, not today! This particular issue was a bit beyond us both.

Having waited impatiently for two weeks, I finally caved and rang Loss Adjuster Number 1 to find that Beloved Husband was entirely correct. (How galling is that?) The Structural Engineer's report was still unavailable. This was nearly two and a half weeks since he had crawled all over the remains of our disintegrating house. How could it possibly take that long for him to write a report?

Immediately after placing (note the impressive physical restraint) down the telephone receiver to Loss Adjuster Number 1, I called the mobile number that Structural Engineer Man had foolishly provided me with, on that day, so long ago, when he had visited our property. I didn't have the time to be patient and just wait and see. That report needed writing.

He answered relatively quickly, I thought (on the twentieth ring), and snuffled down the line at me that he had been ill. I sympathised briefly, with remarkable sincerity, and mentioned that we were still in the tent that he had seen our children erecting when he visited. Including the eldest, who had only recently been discharged from hospital following her latest bout of major abdominal surgery and had fairly significant, mobility problems associated with her recovery. None of which were helped by prolonged tented accommodation. (Well he was the one who introduced health issues into the mix. I was just following his lead.)

Accidental Damage

Was that laying it on bit thick do you think? It was all perfectly true. He was a grown up after all and I didn't think he needed sheltering from the very real situation facing our family.

We needed him to do his job. Things were not going to move forward until he did.

As it was events did stumble forward (or backwards in fact, depending on how you look at it) very shortly afterwards when I received a fleeting telephone call from Loss Adjuster Number 1.

These transitory communications appeared to be his speciality, as were momentary visits to properties for insubstantial meetings it would seem.

I was to wonder later on whether this was a deliberate tactic employed for personal safety reasons in case his clients became unreasonably enraged and attacked him. One should remember he would regularly meet with people enduring all sorts of personal crisis situations and perhaps short encounters limited the chance that he might be verbally or even physically abused whilst performing his duties.

While I definitely understood the impulse to indulge in a bit of verbal abuse, there was absolutely no chance of him being shouted at by me. I had found that a hard constricting lump had settled in the region of my throat and wouldn't be dislodged. This was making breathing, swallowing and talking almost impossible.

My mobile phone rang late one afternoon. It was my day off, and I was sat on the wonky floor upstairs in the master bedroom attempting to dismantle a chest of drawers so that I could fit it down the stairwell. Loss Adjuster Number 1 stayed on the line long enough to laugh jovially as he told me that we were not covered for the structural issues at our property as we didn't have accidental damage cover included in our policy. He would send me an email to confirm.

I listened to the ended call tone for a long time after he had swiftly disconnected. He had hung up so quickly in fact that I hadn't had a chance to speak at all, which was useful really as it spared me the trouble of formulating a response.

Well!

What in earth was Accidental Damage?

Accidental Damage
Definition: damage to an individual's home or its contents that transpires inadvertently during the course of everyday life.

I was quickly to learn that accidental damage is something that you opt into when you take out house insurance. It doesn't come as standard, and basically if you don't have this then you are in trouble. Or at least that is what I understood from the brief call. I may be wrong.

I clearly remember talking to the bright young thing on the phone when setting up our house insurance several years earlier. The conversation was really very speedy. How many bedrooms did the property have? How old was the property, did it have a thatched roof etc....? She spoke incredibly quickly, rattling off reams of information as well as the terms and conditions, which made it all quite hard to follow. I kept on having to ask her to repeat things in an effort to understand. She complied, very patiently, but she seemed completely unable to actually slow down the verbal torrent of information or explain it any other way. In the end she gave me a quote that sounded reasonable and I accepted it.

I certainly don't remember being given the option of having accidental damage and then (wait for it...) *deliberately and actively turning it down*.

But I must have done.

Why on earth would I do that?

I have a highly developed sense of paranoia. If it can go wrong, it definitely will. That is my life.

Added to that, I cohabit with a small tribe of Barbarians. Why on earth would I not take out accidental damage insurance?

9: <u>Courage</u>

Definition: the capacity to do something that terrifies you, fortitude when confronting pain or grief.

Fast forward to present day.....

Finally, painting away in my little study two years later, I was beginning to realise that this particular issue with the insurance was probably the main root of my problem.

Could this really be the reason that I had not been able to forgive myself? Although innocent of the main event, in some respects I had to admit that I had been responsible for a significant element of the subsequent ramifications.

Somehow, in the course of that telephone call to set up our house insurance so many years previously, I must have got it wrong! I had made a mistake that was to affect all my precious people massively and so very detrimentally for months if not years to come, possibly permanently.

Had I genuinely reacted to subconscious guilt by damaging myself so effectively for so long? Punishing myself by intentionally cutting off a major source of comfort because I didn't think I deserved it? Perhaps all this time I was carrying on as if everything was fine, while the hidden cracks in my own personal foundations continued to throb with pain.

The cat gave a jaw-cracking yawn from the window sill, obviously finding my company immensely boring. She lazily turned her back on me while Adele's dulcet tones floated up from the radio.

Accidental Damage

I took a large swig from the cup of tea that sat steaming away unobtrusively at my elbow, next to a large chocolate crispy cake, and wondered.....

***

Looking back at that awful time again I remembered that later that same day, after Loss Adjuster Number 1's phone call, I had been forced to confirm to my Beloved Husband that we were completely on our own. That the house insurance policy, for which we had paid so much over the years, was not going to help us now that we needed it. I remember watching in desperation as the last tiny flicker of hope in his eyes flared briefly before going out.

He is the strong and silent type and didn't say a word of recrimination. Not one to wail and moan at life's problems, he just gets on with what needs to be done. Now, regardless of his personal feelings of despair, not once did he blame me for our predicament. Yet I wondered how I was going to live with myself?

Lying wordlessly side by side with him under a pile of cold, damp duvets in the tent that night, both of us beyond completely exhausted, staring sightlessly up at the canvas roof in shock, I felt as though my heart was being crushed beneath many tonnes of concrete.

I knew that he was there next to me, sharing the heavy weight that was pressing down and I was struck by the supreme contradiction that this represented. The immense comfort of knowing that the person I loved the most was with me, that I wasn't alone in my misery, was countered by the devastating knowledge that not only was he suffering too, but that I had inadvertently added to that suffering.

Had I been given a choice I would simply have turned my face to the wall and died. Yet obviously I couldn't, and now I wonder, is it truly a sad state of affairs when your only will to live is derived purely from the existence of another?

Perhaps not, for in truth my Beloved Husband is the only thing that got me through that awful night, a light in the deepest darkness.

At that moment of utter despair, in a state of complete physical and mental exhaustion, there had been an almost imperceptible rustle, a minor movement as the little finger on his right hand entwined itself with the little finger on my left and held on tight.

***

Returning to the present, I shook myself away from those dark memories and looked at what I had created while my mind wandered through the past.

Ah!

All black!

No, I am not referring to the New Zealand Rugby Team.

My canvas. Ninety by sixty inches of complete and utter black.

Accidental Damage

It's not a nice shiny black either. I had just spent the last hour and a half covering the whole surface in several layers of deep, unrelieved, matt black.

If it was a reflection of my thoughts then perhaps it was apt. That moment in the past when I realised that our appalling situation was my fault had probably been one of the bleakest times for me, especially as I was then finally coming to understand just how momentous the resulting consequences from my mistake might be. (More of that to follow...)

I wondered where I was planning to go with this painting and reached for another pot of paint before forcing my mind back to those terrible times determined that now I had started stirring this whole thing up, I would see it through to the bitter end.

10: <u>Silver lining</u>

Definition: a comforting or positive aspect of an otherwise fraught situation.

Back to the past...

We should consider that the responsibilities of adulthood can frequently make us neglect the true meaning of life as we become swept up in the pursuit of ephemeral goals forgetting to enjoy every moment for what it is.

Taking a lesson from the supreme wisdom of Monty Python, I would suggest that we must attempt to look on the bright side of life, and it would be a major mistake to think that everything about that fateful summer was to be doom and gloom for our intrepid little band, for it most certainly wasn't.

As always, life with the Barbarians was never boring. Over the years it has been a profound privilege to bear witness to them evolving. Observing them throwing themselves into new life experiences with a joyful exuberance has been truly awe inspiring, if simultaneously exhausting and terrifying from a parental perspective.

That summer proved that our Barbarians definitely had living in the moment sussed, possessed as they are of a highly developed sense of the ridiculous leading to frequent burst of hilarity no matter how bleak the prospects around them.

The prolonged period of warm dry weather provided the most delightful of rare but perfect British Summers which resulted in our protracted garden camping existence

Accidental Damage

definitely having its more positive moments. After all we were taking our inspiration from Enid Blyton's Famous Five and camping in the ruins of our home, much as they had camped in the ruins of a Castle in their very first adventure. An Englishman's home and all that, although there were no lashings of ginger beer, we can't stand the stuff.

As soon as the school holidays commenced officially, our Barbarians, the boys in particular, were able to indulge their wilder sides on an almost permanent basis, thoroughly enjoying being out of doors.

The fact that the PlayStation and TV required acts of extreme exertion to access almost all of the time, given the piles of boxes stacked haphazardly every which way in the house, they swiftly ceased trying and instead indulged in their own personal re-enactment of FIFA12 on the muddy patch of ground beneath the oak trees at the bottom of the garden.

Probably the single most enjoyable aspect of this football fest was the careful transfer of the previously mentioned mud from the ground to large areas of their own persons. What could be more fun?

Let's face it people do pay large amounts of money to be covered in mud for health benefits. Could this be a possibility for raising the missing £200,000? We certainly seemed to have an unlimited supply of mud. (Hmm! That's not a bad idea, I think I might start making a list of potential money making schemes.)

The mud, once acquired, was then removed in a somewhat haphazard yet fairly effective manner by chasing each other through the sprinkler in the early evening before the heat of the day waned. Regrettably, the neighbours would be forgiven for thinking our mini marauders were committing multiple acts of murder given the amount of squealing that this activity generated. We are very remote here but there are a few rural properties with the misfortune of living just within earshot of our makeshift encampment. Nevertheless our dear neighbours were very patient through all of the nonsense that went on that summer as well as what was to follow.

At night, though in spite of the bright sunny days, I have to admit that I still felt the cold. Perhaps it was the contrast of the night time temperatures with the daytime warmth. However this didn't seem to affect the Barbarians at all, no doubt helped a little by the hot water bottles I would stuff into their sleeping bags last thing at night while they snored away peacefully, just before I collapsed into my own bed.

Conceivably it was my age that meant I felt the cold more than they did, or maybe it was the chill weight of sheer dread I was carrying around in the core of my being like a block of ice slowly freezing my heart, which made it impossible to warm up.

There is no doubt though, that for the adults, the nights passed in a blur of the following: struggling into a chilly sleeping bag and then trying to insert yourself under several layers of duvets on a slightly damp mattress in order to get to bed in the tent, then lying awake all night feeling cold and worrying; trying to remember to breathe. At three AM most nights I would wonder if I had the energy to keep going. Was I even going to able to get up in the morning? During those long dark nights it definitely felt like it would be a kindness if

Accidental Damage

I could simply choose to never wake up again rather than face the months ahead. Sleep would eventually claim us, but it wasn't the restorative kind.

We would wake up unbelievably early from brief, unrestful slumber and for just a few seconds each morning everything would be alright. Then reality would come crashing back in as we realised that it hadn't all been just a bad dream. Our house genuinely had fallen down, and we truly were living in a tent in the back garden. This was our reality.

Beloved Husband and I would force our aching bodies and bruised spirits upright, to keep going, to survive another minute, then another hour and eventually another day. Pretending to the Barbarian Horde all along that we had slept just fine and wasn't the whole thing just an exciting adventure!

I don't think for one minute that they believed us because frankly we're not very good actors and they are all pretty smart.

In an inspired move, the girls started switching the radio on almost immediately on waking each morning so that the music, the routine of regular traffic and news announcements as well as the light hearted banter between the co-presenters could bring a welcome distraction and a much needed air of normality to our al-fresco early starts.

Chatting away in a studio somewhere, there is no way that those two complete strangers and the production team supporting them could possibly have known what an important lifeline they were throwing to one displaced, desperate little family unit.

Nevertheless in spite of that, trying to accomplish anything at all continued to feel like we were wading through treacle. Slow, painful and messy.

I continued making meals for all but would then just push my portion round my plate. Speaking was hard, swallowing impossible. I wasn't the only one struggling. Beloved Husband was doing the same. Without a single word of reproach sent my way.

All the time we kept reassuring the Barbarian Horde that everything would be OK. They knew we were lying and so did we, but everyone pretended for each other's sake and we just kept calm and carried on wading.

***

Eventually the nice lady who rented the field next door for her horses beckoned to me from her side of the fence.

"What a lovely idea to camp in the garden. Your kids must be having a wonderful time. Aren't you a great mum?" she said.

I think it was probably the parenting compliment that demolished any stiff-upper-lipped pretence on my part that all was hunky dory. I sighed heavily and filled her in, even though I didn't really know her from Eve and she probably wished she had never asked. I had no polite filter in place to be anything but brutally blunt.

House falling down. Potential £200,000 bill or more.

Accidental Damage

House Insurance refusing to have anything to do with it.

Don't know what to do. Shrug!

She seemed genuinely shocked and sympathetic. I did not realise it at the time but this encounter was going to prove to be fairly pivotal for the remainder of my story, but more of that later.

Smiling a sad goodbye I walked away from her towards the sheds at the bottom of the garden and thought no more of it.

****

Now at that time we were desperately in need of storage. Having emptied large amounts from the houses into the garden, we need to get it all sorted and stored before the spell of good weather broke. At this time the useable parts of the house contained piles of boxes of displaced belongings with other larger items in heaps outside on the grass under tarpaulin.

Now that we knew there was definitely no help coming our way from the house insurance we would need to find £200,000 all by ourselves. There would be no extra available to pay for additional storage. The current plan was to sort through everything including the double garage and several sheds to get rid of anything that wasn't absolutely essential so that we could free up space for the things we needed to keep.

Thus began the first of countless trips to the tip, recycling centre and charity shops as much of the family's historic treasures were eliminated.

Looking back on it we probably should have tried to sell some stuff online too, but we didn't have the time, the know-how or a suitably reliable internet connection to achieve this effectively. As it was Beloved Husband sorted the tip items and I arranged the charity shop trips and recycling. Neither option was a walk in the park due to the staggering volume of stuff to be purged.

Understandably, if you take too large a donation to one charity shop the ladies in charge start to get quite twitchy, mainly because they don't usually have room for you to unload your entire house into their little stockroom cupboards.

I began to take longer and longer trips out, combing local towns and villages for charity shops that I had yet to donate to. Feeling immensely embarrassed, I would walk in quickly and leave several bags of good quality items before trying to escape as fast as possible before some sweet old lady could ask me about gift aiding. Not that I normally minded gift aiding, I just found that my voice wasn't co-operating which made communication of any sort very difficult. I had also been warned that apparently you can only gift aid so much before the tax man starts getting stroppy and believe me I had enough problems on my plate without upsetting Her Majesty's Revenue & Customs.

Similarly if you turn up at the tip too often they start getting suspicious and think you are dumping stuff from a business, or perhaps operating as a professional house clearer, on the

Accidental Damage

sly. (Now there's another idea for earning the extra £200,000. I am on a role here!)

Beloved Husband finally started a bonfire at the bottom of the garden in order to burn what rubbish we could in order to save on the sheer number of tip trips. The Barbarians had leapt on the idea and thoroughly enjoyed throwing on things like old card board, broken chests of drawers, piles of school jotters and exercise books. (I promise that we checked they were the old ones before allowing them to do this.) Eventually they chucked in huge foil-wrapped packages of potatoes with chunks of butter inside and also cored apples stuffed with raisins and syrup, to be raked from the ashes later and consumed whilst we all sat on or around the old swings in the sunset.

Ultimately though, we exhausted the tip, fire and charity shop options and what remained were all the items we needed to keep and therefore to store.

The sheds and the garage (Beloved Husband has collected a fair number of sheds over the years fortunately) had all been cleared of unnecessary junk and our more essential possessions stored carefully in the space created.

This work was achieved in silence.

There was nothing to say.

It wasn't an angry, accusatory silence; it was merely an empty exhausted one.

Talking would require oxygen and there simply didn't seem to be enough of that. Every breath required supreme effort.

We just had to keep putting one foot in front of the other in that deep, ever present treacle. This was merely the first of so many tasks that we were going to have to complete in order to move forward.

The sorting process, in its entirety, took several solid weeks of hard work interspersed with actually going to work and trying to keep our jobs. During this time Beloved Husband periodically disappeared into the house to rummage around inside the computer, investigating our finances and exploring options for locating £200,000.

On one such occasion, left alone in the garden, I approached my little wooden summer house (in other words, a shed with a slightly bigger window than normal) and unlocked the door. Inside was my sanctuary, my painting space crammed with all my work, stacked neatly after my latest exhibition. My favourite pieces were on the walls but a relatively large storage area would be available if I moved all the other paintings out.

For the first time in weeks I felt something other than emptiness and despair. Here was something I could do. A tiny thing in relation to the problems before us but at least this was one issue within my power at last. We needed space.

I could create a bit of space. Right here, right now.

Before I could stop myself I had started to haul canvasses roughly out on to the grass. It wasn't long before I couldn't stop myself from throwing them onto the nearby bonfire.

Accidental Damage

Huge paintings, one after the other, crashed into the flames while I stood and watched.

A strange thing happened.

Gone was the anaesthetising numbness in which I had been, barely, existing and in its place was genuine sensation. Admittedly it was unbelievably painful at first, but weirdly, it was good to feel something, anything at all. In some ways the pain helped. I deserved to suffer for my mistakes. If I had not been distracted with my paintings all the time, so obsessed with getting back to them, then perhaps I wouldn't have made that disastrous mistake when I was setting up the house insurance. If I'd paid attention to more important things then maybe we would be fully covered. Maybe everything would have been alright.

I threw another painting to join the others in the growing inferno.

At least I was feeling something legitimate at last. I was so angry with myself. It was the very first spark that would eventually become a seething anger that was to mature and develop into a raging fury, one that I could eventually turn outwards and use to get us all through this. A force to be reckoned with! When I was ready, anyone who got in my way was going to seriously regret it.

Beloved Husband came running out of the house. (Anyone except him of course.)

"What are you doing?" he asked in astonishment. "You don't have to do that, we'll find somewhere for them."

"There is nowhere else. I am just being practical. They aren't likely to sell at the moment anyway. The downturn in the market has affected everyone. People just aren't buying art anymore. We don't have the luxury of space right now so let's get rid of them. It's more important that we sort our home out for our children."

"At least keep some," he insisted. "Surely there's no need to destroy them all?"

"Yes there is" I replied and flung yet another canvas into the flames. "There's every need."

PART 3

Legend states that the phoenix must burn before it can rise from the ashes reborn.

11: <u>Millstone</u>

Definition: rounded stone used for grinding, or alternatively a weighty load that crushes.

Returning to the present.......

I resurfaced in my little study and looked at the canvas before me.

"That's interesting!" I thought looking at the dark display. Not quite so black as it had been though.

Of course that was before I looked at my watch and realised I was late to pick up the Barbarian Horde. Oooops! Very late!

I threw a large cloth over the easel to hide the painting. I was going to need to think about this before I let anyone see it.

Hurling myself into the car I sped off to retrieve the tribe from their establishments of enlightenment and returned shortly thereafter to throw tea at them, (not literally, although sometimes it is tempting). Then I fed the dishwasher and the washing machine, before setting off yet again to post appropriate people to the various after school activities on the schedule for that evening.

Driving along humming to the radio I caught Quiet's eye in the rear view mirror. He was grinning smugly to himself.

"What?" I asked.

Accidental Damage

"Told you you'd be less grumpy."

He wouldn't say that if he could see the sinister, metallic sunflower I had just painted on that huge black canvas. It really was quite psychotic. Perhaps I should hide it somewhere very permanent so that no one could decide I needed carting off to the funny farm for a lengthy stay of respite care. They might never let me out.

I felt absolutely and completely fine, but that didn't mean my behaviour, or my artwork, matched.

The next day though I was surprised to acknowledge that I had slept extremely well, probably for the first time in ages, and I wondered if the act of creating these rather menacing images had in fact allowed me to express feelings that I couldn't speak about aloud, feelings that had hung on me like a heavy millstone for a very long time.

"Who needs a psychiatrist when you've got a large canvas, a ready supply of Daler Rowney and a four inch brush?" I thought to myself, in amusement.

Better out than in I supposed.

Might as well see where it took me. Anything was worth a try in order to get a good night's sleep around here.

It so happened that I had two weeks of time-owing from my job that needed using up.

You know what employers are like, they tell you that you can take 20 days annual leave and then throw so many projects at you that actually taking the time off is extremely difficult.

Then at the end of the year they say that as you haven't taken the time off you obviously enjoy your job so much that you didn't need it and then they take the days you haven't used away from you because it's now a new financial year (as if that matters).

Ok I will admit there is probably some sensible business reason for not being able to carry over annual leave into the next year. It's the same where I work if you do unpaid overtime. You have to take any unpaid overtime back pretty sharpish or it gets forgotten. I was determined not to lose my time off and so had taken the next two weeks off work even though no one else in the family was going to be around to share them with me.

Occupational options for today included numerous housekeeping tasks, none of which I had any intention of attempting. I had decided that I was going to paint again. All day! Perhaps all this thinking back though old events was doing me some good.

As I dressed, I pulled on my favourite comfort jumper as a talisman. It was an old one of my mother's that she'd been about to throw out two years ago, but as she knew I had always liked it, she had offered it to me first. My Ancient Parents (A.P.s for short) are not, in fact, remotely ancient, I just call them that to wind them up.

The A.P.s had been most concerned to hear of the disaster that had befallen our lovely, rustic home but as they lived in deepest darkest Devon, some three hours away by car, they were unable to be of much practical or financial help. Believe me we are not the sort of family that has a spare £200,000 plus lying around, although if they did I know they would have offered it. As would Beloved Husband's parents had they been able.

All the A.P.s could really do was to patiently listen for hours as I sobbed down the phone and I was grateful for that.

Having suggested that I meet them half way for lunch so that they could reassure themselves that I wasn't about to top myself, they fed me, dried my tears and handed me mum's old jumper which I immediately put on. I didn't take it off for days because it smelled like my childhood home (she hasn't changed her washing powder in all this time) a scent I still associate with being protected and safe. It felt like a permanent parental hug and I needed all the comfort I could get.

Ultimately though after about a week it started to smell like mouldy old tents and even though people expect you to whiff a bit if you are camping out, I finally gave in and washed it, putting it back on immediately it was dry.

It is still my favourite item of comfort clothing today even though it is getting extremely thread bare. As such, it seemed fitting to wear it now as I planned to return to face the demons of the past.

Speaking of demons, the Barbarians needed relocating back to school before I could have the luxury of rummaging through my memories again.

12: <u>Fairy Godmother</u>

Definition: a person who comes to the assistance of someone in trouble.

Back in the past...

As I understand it, Fairy Godmothers come in many different forms and have a habit of popping up when you least expect them. Cinderella didn't recognise hers when she appeared disguised as an old crone at the kitchen door before the ball, and two years ago, I certainly didn't expected mine to arrive wearing muddy Hunters and a battered Barbour jacket over a smart business suit. But there you are. Life is full of surprises!

In the interest of political correctness I should probably refer to this welcome visitor as a Fairy Godperson, even though my spellcheck doesn't like it, and if I wished to be totally fair, perhaps I should drop the 'fairy' bit too as there were no signs of wings, wand or anything else and I wouldn't want to be sued for slander.

Never mind, I am sure that you get the general idea. All I am trying to say is that a benevolent stranger turned up completely out of the blue and tried to help.

I am referring to the day after my major oil paint fuelled bonfire, when the lady who owned the horses in the field next door hailed me for a second time. I was engaged in raking over the smouldering bonfire ashes. (Do please note the continuing Cinderella analogy here. I am rather proud of it.) At the same time I was contemplating the steely determination to take action that had been forged in my heart while I watched my artwork burn.

The only problem was that I wasn't exactly sure what action to take.

Putting the rake to one side and dusting ash off my hands I ambled over to the fence, expecting some more sympathy but she was eminently more practical and briskly introduced me to her husband (who was wearing the afore-mentioned Hunters and Barbour jacket). "I hope you don't mind, but I told my husband what you said yesterday. He says he's got some information you might find useful."

I shook hands and smiled politely.

"I don't mean to intrude, but I couldn't believe what my wife told me yesterday. It is so staggeringly awful."

I nodded in agreement.

"I know there is probably nothing practical we can do to help you so I've made a few enquiries instead," he continued. "Don't worry I kept it all anonymous. Just asked theoretical questions, you know? I don't deal with insurance myself, but I work with a lot of people who do. Did you know that you can reject the house insurance company's decision?"

I shook my head, wondering precisely where he was going with this.

"Are you actually sure you are not covered? Have you looked at your detailed policy document? After all they might just have made a mistake? Overlooked something?

Have you read the small print?" he asked intently. I stared blankly at him, trying to keep up.

"Look, tell me if I am teaching my grandmother to suck eggs," he continued hurriedly, obviously keen not to have offended me. "You and your husband are probably dealing with all of this very competently, but it just seems unbelievable that you can simply have the door shut in your face like that. It has to be a mistake, surely?"

I didn't like to mention that my Beloved Husband was currently busy practising his excellent verbally-challenged-ostrich impressions and I wasn't sure he was competently dealing with breathing let alone anything else.

I also resisted pointing out that I was a strong, independent woman and could sort my own problems out without a man. Mainly because right then I wasn't, and I couldn't, so I didn't.

This really nice, compete stranger was genuinely trying to help and I was very grateful indeed.

"I looked at the insurance certificate," I said, struggling to get my rusty voice to work after a period of disuse. "They are right, we haven't got accidental damage."

"But you have got basic house insurance haven't you?" he insisted patiently. I have to admit I wasn't in great shape for processing any information at that point so he could be forgiven for thinking that I was a bit dim.

I nodded.

Accidental Damage

"Ok, good, so you just haven't got accidental damage. Well what's accidental about this whole thing?" he asked. "Who decided it was an accident? And why? You didn't accidentally do something like drive into your own house did you?"

He stopped and looked uncertainly at me for a moment. "You didn't, did you?"

I shook my head. "Of course not," I replied. "The cob gave way, apparently it can do that, but I have no idea why."

"Well then. Accidental damage is only a small part of house insurance. You need to find out what you are covered for. Otherwise what on earth have you been paying them for? You took out a policy with them in good faith. You trusted them to sell you something that would protect your home for you and your children. You had every reason to believe that you were covered. They have a duty of care towards you that is not being met. You must go back to them. Start asking questions. Get them to listen to you. Fight back."

He was getting quite frustrated with me now and, from a logical point of view, understandably so. However, in my defence, unless you have actually been in our position no one could possibly understand how helpless and feeble a previously active, dynamic and relatively intelligent person can become when faced with such catastrophe.

It was true though, that at that point in time Beloved Husband and I had simply accepted the primary decision as final and given up. We had absolutely no idea how to move forward.

We were both in shock at losing our home, and utterly terrified about the potential consequences of this disaster to our growing family. In that paralysed state we were really not capable of making important decisions.

We both oscillated between sitting in a heap and staring into space for ages (trying not to cry, in my case) sometimes rocking silently or twitching uncontrollably, while at other times we were manically working on emptying damaged rooms and storing salvageable items, all the time lying cheerfully to the Barbarians saying that everything was going to be just fine. Not that they believed us.

"But how?" I asked eventually.

"Refuse to accept their decision, write back to them saying they are wrong and must reconsider. If they still refuse to help you then you can go to the financial ombudsman, but you have to go back to the insurance company first. They have to have turned you down a second time before the financial ombudsman will look at your case, but there is a real chance that the financial ombudsman will rule in your favour."

I didn't like to ask what the financial ombudsman was. I had never heard of or needed one until now. I made a mental note to google it. I nodded slowly trying to think through the thick fog of tiredness that was smothering my brain.

"What have you got to lose?" he asked. "It can't get any worse can it?"

Now there's a silly question! Things can always get worse....

13: <u>Guardian Angel</u>

Definition: A person or spirit that watches over protectively.

Still in the past...

Up until then we had enjoyed clear skies and warm balmy days. Unusually for Britain this occurred during the first few weeks of the school summer holidays and the whole country basked in sunshine as we toiled at our salvage operation.

You might be interested to know that the nights in the tent were still very cold though in spite of the mini heat wave that was roasting the daytime hours. Or have I mentioned that already? We had managed to drag several mattresses out of the house and inserted them with considerable difficulty into the sleeping compartments of the tent followed by a selection of sleeping bags, blankets and duvets. These, coupled with the aforementioned hot water bottles, full nightwear, fleeces, dressing gowns and woolly hats made up our night time attire. I drew the line at wearing a coat to bed although I did seriously consider it at one point.

Each evening started out sufficiently snug and then slowly deteriorated as the darkness deepened, into a series of hours in which one debated whether getting up to put on yet another layer of clothing would result in too much body heat being lost in the process or would staying still and ignoring the increasing chill be a better option? (I never did work out the answer to that one.)

This was inevitably followed by pondering whether one needed to go to the loo sufficiently badly to warrant the effort involved in extracting oneself from sleeping bag and tent to trot across the garden into the house, waking everyone up in the process (why are tent zips so noisy?) and once again losing all body heat into the bargain.

Added to these personal night time deliberations I also felt obliged to accompany Small, the youngest Barbarian, into the house whenever he required the bathroom, because I reasoned that, as he was only seven, it was unacceptable to let him cross the garden and enter a house with stability issues, in the dark, on his own.

What disaster might befall him on this quick journey (the loo is right by the back door after all and the tent was very close to the house)was undetermined, but, as I am sure I have mentioned previously, I am blessed with a highly developed sense of paranoia that had not been helped by recent events. Now might be the exact time that savage wolves or grizzly bears decided to announce their secretly re-introduced presence in Britain, just in time to snaffle a sleepy seven-year-old-boy-sized snack.

Of course once all these night time issues have been endured, it should be remembered precisely how early the day starts when you are camping, especially in summer. Dawn is volubly welcomed shortly after 4am by the birds, making the nights so short that really there was no time to grumble about the lack of sleep before it was time to get up again.

As it happened, Chaos had found it impossible to negotiate the tent as a sleeping accommodation option due to her

Accidental Damage

'recently-discharged-from-hospital-following-major-surgery' condition (stitches, four hourly requirements for medication taken with food, post-operative pain, and mobility issues will do that). As a result she stayed in the house for the nights. Those mattresses that we had been unable to stuff into the tent were piled up along the far wall in the lounge area and she had made herself a cosy nest on the top like some modern day princess and the pea.

Of course my paranoia came into play here as well as I was convinced that given Chaos' above-mentioned 'recently-discharged-from-hospital-following-major-surgery' condition, she shouldn't really be in the house on her own in case she fell or suffered a relapse and required rescuing.

OK, I agree, I was definitely looking for trouble now as at 17 years old she was perfectly capable of looking after herself, or at least ringing my mobile if she had a problem, but give me a break! These were very extenuating circumstances. After all there was still a blooming great hole in our wall that would not stop strange people (or their dogs) from wandering in off the street without so much as a by-your-leave.

The result was that I spent most of the nights wandering from tent to house and back again checking that my chickens were all present and correct, whilst systematically putting on any number of additional layers of clothing. No wonder I was behaving strangely.

Then the weather broke and things got worse.

This was, without a doubt, the moment when my dread of storms was born.

Alice May

The night following my encounter with my fairy godparent (or whatever we decided he was) the good weather announced an abrupt departure in truly spectacular fashion. In came the rain with a vengeance. As if to punish us for the unaccustomed sunshine, water fell in torrents, making trips between tent and house extremely unpleasant. Nevertheless we persevered. What choice did we have?

Even after that first flash of lightning followed almost immediately by a deafening crack of thunder, right over head. There we were, frozen with shock into our sleeping bags.

The most colossal thunderstorm was upon us so quickly, that there was very little time to consider where the safest place to be actually was. It was definitely not in a flimsy tent pitched underneath a large oak tree. Then again, it probably also wasn't in a crumbly, old thatched property encased in countless long metal scaffolding poles and other excellent lightening conductors either.

The next crack of thunder decided it and once the first of us had made a break for the house the rest of us didn't hang about. Fortunately, as the last one out, I did remember to zip up the tent behind me in a somewhat vain attempt to keep all the abandoned bedding dry. (Or do I just mean 'less wet'?)

The Princess of Chaos had descended from her mattress tower and met us at the conservatory doors with a strong torch and some thick towels.

Accidental Damage

"I wondered how long you'd last out there in this," she said handing the towels over. "It's probably a bit dodgy to have electric stuff on in here, so I turned off all the lights, unplugged the computer and TV and found a few torches. I also think it might be a good idea to get the fire going for heat as well as light. That way we don't increase our chances of attracting a stray lightning bolt given our current circumstances. It's not like we are going to get much sleep with this going on anyway."

(I am sorry, but who kidnapped the Princess of Chaos and replaced her with Captain Sensible?)

Not to be outdone, Logic started shifting the piles of boxes around. "If we shove all this out of the way we could move the sofa over and put some of Chaos' pile of mattresses down by the fire. We are going to need some rest, even if we can't sleep. It'll be nice and cosy soon, probably the warmest night we've had for a few weeks."

In the end we decided to block up the back door by the bathroom with the boxes as there was nowhere else to put them. After all we weren't actually using the back door just then and if we needed to get out in a hurry the conservatory doors were so much closer.

(You see we were all thinking like proper paranoids now.)

It is very true though that it is an ill wind that blows no one any good. We were surprisingly comfortable, snuggled up on mattresses by the fire as the storm raged outside. It wasn't long before Small fell into a deep sleep as demonstrated by some rather remarkable snoring. As for the rest of us there was a powerful sense of security and reassurance in staying together and looking after each other. I would pin point that night as being one when perhaps healing began. Admittedly the wound that had been dealt to our home and family life was hideous but we were actually surviving spectacularly well under the circumstances.

As sleep was out of the question (given the combined impact of storm and the seven year old's snores) we eventually started to chat amongst ourselves, something that there hadn't really been time for in recent weeks. The conversation inevitably turned to our situation and I made the mistake of suggesting that perhaps given the stormy weather forecast for the week ahead, we should take the A.P.s up on their offer to house the children in their spare room in Devon, at least for the rest of the summer holidays. Beloved Husband's parents had also kindly offered to help out in a similar way.

The atmosphere in the cosy room changed instantly and the three wakeful Barbarians looked at me reproachfully in chilly silence.

"What?" I asked.

"You are kidding right?" Such immediate eloquence from Quiet rather indicated his strength of feeling on the matter of an imminent departure for Devon.

Then the others waded into the fray.

"Like that's happening!" snorted the Princess of Chaos delicately.

Accidental Damage

"You are always telling us that if we stick together we can do anything," said Logic, "and now at the first sign of trouble you are telling us to abandon ship. I wish you would make your mind up!"

The first sign of trouble?

Seriously?

Did she genuinely think this lightning storm was the *first* sign? I think we were well past sign number one, don't you?

"Anyway Granma doesn't have a PlayStation," said Quiet as if that concluded the arguments for the defence. Wow two statements from him in less than two minutes! He obviously had fairly intense feelings on the matter.

It was an established fact that the rest of the house could crumble to dust for all the boys would care as long as the lounge remained intact so they could play FIFA. (Note the PlayStation was now accessible since moving all those boxes to the back door, a fact that had been carefully observed by Small before he fell asleep.)

It would appear that our mini marauders were staging a mutiny.

Unexpectedly my Beloved Husband leapt immediately to my defence.

"Your mother is only trying to keep you safe," he said quietly. "I don't think you realise just how scared we both are that if we send you to grandparents, no matter how temporarily, we might not get you back any time soon.

We are in serious trouble here. You three are old enough to understand that surely?

As your parents we have a duty to supply a safe home for you all, and we are currently failing to do that. If social services find out, they could take you all away and put you in care.

The house insurance have refused to help us, we have barely any savings after the last lot of building work we paid for and I can't ask the mortgage company to lend us any more money on credit because when I enquired about it they said that they would want to do a drive by to check the condition of the property before agreeing to anything. As the house is currently, very obviously, a wreck then they will understandably refuse and might start to question the security of the existing mortgage. Maybe even call it in.

We can't sell the property as it is as we will make a massive loss because it is currently only worth a fraction of its true value in this condition. We can't go into hotels or rented accommodation, because everywhere is booked solid till late-September.

Believe me when I say that I have looked at all of these options in detail. Unfortunately we have no money available to pay for any of them."

We all looked at him, stunned by the sheer number of words coming out of his mouth after such a long period of silence. Obviously a great deal more than any of us had suspected had been going on inside his head whilst he had had it

Accidental Damage

figuratively buried in the sand during all those incredibly outstanding mute ostrich impressions.

He wasn't finished yet.

"The only reason we haven't had to send you away up until now is the fact that it is the summer holidays and camping in the garden is a perfectly acceptable thing to do as a holiday occupation. People pay a fortune for that sort of torture, especially round here.

But come September when school starts again, then we have to have adequate accommodation for you. There is a very real possibility that we'll have to enrol you in schools near your grandparents or your aunts' and uncles' homes so that you can continue your education in a proper environment while your mother and I fix this mess.

We can't even guarantee that you will be able to stay together as there are so many of you. At least we have kind relatives, that we know would treat you well, who have asked if they can help, even if they live so far away.

We also have wonderful friends locally, who I know would offer to have you, but I can't think of anyone who would have space for all of you together, let alone for months on end. Even if our friends can offer to put you up, there is the potential for our misfortune to then damage their family life, which is unthinkable. How can we ask them to do that? It wouldn't be fair to anyone.

As an extreme worst case scenario, there is a very real danger that the State might step in, taking you away from us to put you in care. You might all be placed in different foster homes. We may never be allowed to regain custody of any of you again.

So, however you look at this situation, unless we can find a workable solution, quickly, our family unit, the six of us, will be a thing of the past.

That is what is breaking your mother's heart."

I shuffled closer to him, tucked my arm through his and rested my head on his shoulder before adding quietly, "And your father's."

Now some people might say at this point that we were over-reacting. You might think that such a scenario would never be allowed to happen. To those of you who think that, I can say only this: I never for one second thought my house would fall down. From that moment onwards I will never ever think that something terrible could not happen.

Believe me, anything is possible! Unfortunately!

There was a lengthy silence while the Barbarians digested Beloved Husband's words.

Then:

"As I said," stated the Princess of Chaos defiantly. "That's not happening! You two won't last five minutes without us to look after you. You need us. So, basically we have less than four weeks left and we need a plan. Forget sending us away for now, and let's be practical. What are we going to do?"

Accidental Damage

"Yes, we can help," said Logic.

"Well, I am all out of ideas and totally open to suggestions, so go for it team," Beloved Husband shrugged.

There was silence.

"Um," I said tentatively, wondering absently when exactly he and I had stopped being the ones in charge. "There is one thing," and leaving out all references to fairy godparents, I relayed the information I had learned the previous day.

"That sounds interesting," said the Princess of Chaos pulling her laptop out of a bag near the sofa and booting it up. "Let's put 'financial ombudsman' into a search engine and see what comes up."

"And 'Accidental Damage', see what you can get on that. While she's communing with the internet let's take a look at the small print in those house insurance documents," said Logic.

Beloved Husband was way ahead of her and already digging in the filing cabinet that was wedged at an odd angle between an armchair and the piano. (I told you the rooms had been emptied in a rush.) The cabinet had a couple of printers, a wilting pot plant and a sleeping cat balanced precariously on top.

The cat! Just who had been feeding the cat? I had totally forgotten about her in the last few weeks! What a dreadful owner I was. Still she looked happy enough so someone must have remembered, unless she was catching mice of course.

"I can't believe you haven't done this already!" Logic continued exasperatedly.

She had a point.

And so it was that our own personal choir of guardian angels rallied round to organise their rather shell-shocked parents into developing a plan of action.

14: <u>Healing</u>

Definition: the process of becoming strong or complete again.

Returning to the present ....

Returning to my little study in the future I sensed that the tenor of my painting was changing. Was the initial irrational, 'edge of madness' feeling to my artwork possibly disappearing? I felt the darkness was beginning to show signs of fading. One might even go so far as to suggest that if this continued they might soon start to look relatively sane.

I have heard it said that you have to suffer for true art. If this is what they meant by that, then I really wouldn't recommend it.

Thinking back, Beloved Husband explaining to our older children what the true cost of the loss of the house might mean, had finally dragged the shapeless, nameless monster that was haunting us both, out into the light so that we could see it clearly. This enabled us to start working together to find a way to beat it. To overcome the paralysing power it had over us. The Barbarians' determination not to be sent away but to stay and fight for our way of life alongside us, gave us the additional strength we needed to hold on and focus on a solution to the problem.

We were still a staggeringly long way off success but the first tentative steps were being taken. The burden of responsibility was shared and became lighter with teamwork.

Our little clan truly had its' back to the wall but we were stronger together. Standing shoulder to shoulder against adversity, we were going to come out fighting.

Suddenly, an image that I remembered from before this whole fiasco started, danced across my mind. A concept that had been dreamed up during the long hours sat in hospital waiting rooms with the Princess of Chaos. The existence of this idea was one that I had resolutely denied for nearly three years, closing my thoughts off to it each time it had tried to resurface. I used to tell myself that I didn't do art any more. Yet, now, here I was surrounded by painting materials.

Looking at my watch I realised there was no time to start on anything new right now as parental duties were calling (and also my feet had gone to sleep so I thought I had better walk around to wake them up a bit before I had to drive anywhere). I contented myself with grabbing my last blank canvas and inserting it into the easel for next time. Perhaps I would try something a little different with this old idea and see where my new style would take it.

But for now I had my Barbarian Horde's relentless food requirements to facilitate and I cheerfully set out to the supermarket with a lightness of heart that I was truly grateful for.

I should probably confess here that motherhood did not come as easily to me as I had naively expected it to. Right from the very beginning it wasn't quite what I had imagined. The babies were amazingly wonderful (just as expected), if somewhat noisy. It was me that was the problem. I failed quite miserably to do the most fundamental things like breast feeding. It's a lot harder than you'd think. I was forced to resort to the dreaded bottle after only five days. (No! Not alcohol. Formula!)

Feeding continued to be an issue even when we progressed to solids. I spent days pureeing cooked vegetables (yes, yes, I know about freezing it all in conveniently sized ice cube containers too – it all sounds so eminently reasonable and easy) only to have my little food critics spit it all back at me, so I made the heretical decision to resort to those handy little baby ready meals in tiny tins and jars. It must be remembered that this was way before the lovely, healthy, organic, easy open sachets you see in the stores today, so my baby Barbarians were packed full of preservatives from a very early age. Which does explain a lot!

Understandably to some people, of course, this means that I am totally worthless as a mother and should be taken out immediately and shot. Not surprisingly, I don't subscribe to that theory. Life is hard enough so let's allow ourselves to take the little shortcuts that work for us and run with them.

Luckily, with increasing age, my Barbarians have developed fractionally more healthy food preferences and ready meals no longer feature on the menu. I spend a great deal of time generating colossal quantities of edible offerings from scratch, packed full of nutritional goodness, to put before the tribe. Gratifyingly all is generally demolished in the blink of an eye.

On a good day this is achieved with full use of table manners and 'team-clearing-up' activities afterwards. (Good Parenting Points to be allocated here please!?)

Regrettably, it is usually only ten to fifteen minutes before the little savages (usually, but not always, the boys) start wandering round again looking for more sustenance, which could leave a lesser parent than I feeling quite despondent with the knowledge that she has yet again failed to fulfil her basic nutritional supply duties. I got over that particular guilt-fest a long time ago. Three meals a day is what I signed up for, after that they are on their own. Ish!

My solution has been to designate several large, low level cupboards as acceptable foraging ground. I attempt to keep them packed with accessible, mostly healthy (but not always, depends how desperate I am getting) snacks and they make a sustained attempt to empty them on a regular basis. The situation is assisted by Logic's handy obsession with baking. She has simply trained me to regularly supply basic ingredients for all main cookie / cake options in her repertoire.

Honour is satisfied all round and a degree of parent versus Barbarian balance is achieved as long as I can get to the supermarket before closing time. (It's the country, for goodness sake; there are no 24 hour opening times here, of course it's difficult, but a deal is a deal. Anything worth doing is worth doing well.)

Fortuitously, at this precise moment in time, the supermarkets are currently open because Mother Hubbard has more sustenance in her cupboards than I do right now, so a swift 'smash and grab' is in order at the local food emporium.

15:Treatise

Definition: a methodical discussion or argument in writing including a systematic account of facts, concepts involved and conclusions reached.

And so we return to our adventurers in the past.....

It can be a bit like busses really (not round here of course because there aren't any, it's too remote you see). I am talking about luck. You can have all this rotten luck going on and then all of a sudden several fortuitous things can happen. Like the advent of my fairy godparent.

The trick is to recognise the stroke of good luck when it happens and then make full use of it.

During one of my less frequent forays into the damaged section of the house I happened to notice (Yes! Ok, I admit I was looking through the crack in the wall.) a man standing still at the edge of our driveway with his arms crossed over his chest, having a jolly good look at the house. Now this wasn't that unusual. Not a lot happens in the country entertainment-wise you see and it was currently our turn to amuse everyone. Every Tom, Dick and Aunt Sally had trotted along the lane for a bit of what my father would term 'nosy-parkering'. No one actually meant any harm, so we generally just smiled and waved before carrying on with what we were doing.

Our lovely neighbours had all popped along at some point to sympathise and let us know that if we needed anything we had only to ask. This was extremely kind of them but unfortunately the solution to this particular issue wasn't quite the same as borrowing a cup of sugar or some tea bags. Not many people have a warm, dry home for six going spare. So, while it was fantastic to know that people wished to help, we were all pretty powerless in this scenario which is not a nice feeling for anyone.

We had put up numerous signs and a lot of red tape to indicate to those passing by that the site was dangerous and not actually a new amusement park. We strongly suggested that close proximity to the walls be avoided, because we were a bit concerned that we might get sued if any of our new fans got too near and were injured by falling masonry. (Nanny State and all that, you can't just say that it's someone's own fault they got hurt because they went near an obviously unstable structure anymore.)

Added to that there were several incidents of people driving past and trying to look at the damage to the cottage at same time. This frequently resulted in the rubber-neckers' cars landing in the rather deep ditch on the sharp bend just along the road from the house. It turned out that the local farmer was making a tidy profit hauling these vehicles out with his tractor on a regular basis. (I missed a trick there I should have sent the Barbarians along to help so they could claim a share of the profits. After all, I have £200,000 to find, remember!)

This was different however. I recognised this particular nosy-parker and I wanted a word with him. How fortuitous!

Hopping through the wall (It's quite useful having a hole there when you are in a hurry, not that I am recommending that you get one of course!) I scurried over to him.

Accidental Damage

A tall, good looking, muscular man in his prime, he frowned down at me in a concerned fashion. "Should you be doing that?" he rumbled at me in a deeply reassuring, bass voice. "It looks rather dangerous!"

I looked back over my shoulder at the gap in my lopsided house and shrugged. "Probably not, but it saves ever such a lot of time."

After passing a few pleasantries back and forth, he finally nodded at the house and said, "Not looking too smart is it? Still, I've seen worse."

I was surprisingly torn by his comment. Part of me was reassured that he didn't think things were too bad. Yet, at the same time, a tiny piece of me was also mortally offended that he didn't think my tumble down cottage was absolutely the most impressive tumble down property he had ever seen in his life. (Please note that I do not think I was behaving entirely rationally at this point!)

Nevertheless this was the opening I was waiting for, "Did you know that the insurance assessor is saying it's all because the roof is too heavy. Can you believe that?" I asked with studied care and stepped back slightly to observe his response with interest.

He didn't disappoint me.

I should explain for clarity, at this point, that the man I was talking to, had actually been personally involved in the construction of the very roof that was being blamed by the house insurance's Structural Engineer.

Periodically old thatched rooftops need completely replacing with new timbers and fresh thatch etc. This had last been done just as the gentleman before me was starting out as a very Junior Roofing Apprentice in the family firm.

Nowadays he had a very well-deserved reputation for being absolutely the best Master Roofer for miles around and you could forgive his outrage at the mere suggestion that one of his works of art had actually damaged a property.

I must admit that he displayed a most impressive command of ancient Anglo-Saxon in response to my comment about the house insurance report. This colourful invective was not aimed at me, personally, you understand, the poor chap was venting in the general direction of Structural Engineer Man, who (fortunately for both of them) was not present. This descriptive verbiage was immediately followed by a very detailed and specific description of exactly why the roof couldn't possibly have caused damage like that observed before us. (I won't mention where Master Roofer felt Structural Engineer Man should insert his report. I think you can probably guess.)

Having not really understood much of what he had just said (apart from the last bit of course) I offered him a nice cup of tea. I felt it would help with the shock of having had his work disparaged, so I tentatively took the arm of this enormously cross gentleman and steered him around to the back of the cottage where I parked him on a comfortable seat in the conservatory with a restorative brew. Then, armed with pen and paper, I asked him to repeat exactly what he had said before (not including the Anglo-Saxon bit or the other bit about where to shove.....oh, you know what I mean!) so I could write it all down.

Accidental Damage

In the end I showed him the email that I had received from Loss Adjuster Number 1 in its entirety and he was able to categorically discredit everything mentioned in it using impressively technical roof-building jargon that I could never have made up in a million years. By the time he had finished venting his outrage a large proportion of my letter rejecting the Insurance Company's decision had been created.

Then he said something that was to prove even more note-worthy.

I opened the biscuit tin, sending a small thankful prayer to heaven that the Barbarians had somehow left the contents unmolested, and set it on the table before him, picking up my pen again.

It stands to reason that, as a Master Roofer, my new best friend would also be very experienced in dealing with old buildings in general.

Now, it would seem that the previous winter had been one of the wettest on record for the country and like many others I had watched news reports in horror as large swathes of the next county disappeared under rising flood water. So many people were facing the loss of their homes, something I now had a little more experience of. As it was, we had been in no danger of flooding here but we had still endured massive amounts of rain falling under the action of extreme winds.

Master Roofer pointed out that cob cottages do not generally have foundations, and are therefore in danger of their footings being washed out should they experience significant storm conditions over a prolonged period of time. Such an event would precipitate the sudden collapse of a cob wall.

Aha. How interesting!

One word in particular, stood out.

Storm.

We might not have accidental damage cover, but we certainly had buildings insurance for storm damage. I had seen it in black and white by the light of a flickering fire at four that morning.

A slow smile spread across my face. This just might be the key to moving forward. I believed that I potentially had all the ingredients I needed to put a reasonable request to the house insurance company to reconsider their position on our claim.

I was ready to start fighting back now and, armed with my newly discovered core of steel, I started to do some investigation. Countless research papers, several lengthy telephone conversations and reams of wind speed data and rainfall statistics later, it turned out that there had been more than four major, well documented storm events that previous winter. The last of which had occurred only six weeks prior to the cottage walls failing.

One storm had been identified by the Met Office as the most significant storm to occur in the previous 250 years. A second one had been reported as being worse than the storms of 1987. A third was termed the most noteworthy in

Accidental Damage

40 years. One local planner informed me that there were at least two other cob cottages within a five mile radius of us that had been significantly influenced by storm damage. Fortunately for them, neither of these two was affected to the degree of actual collapse like ours was.

The most prominent part of our cottage, the section that was most exposed to the prevailing winds and unprecedented driving rainfall, the section which had taken the brunt of all these significant storm events, was the corner section between the two walls that had failed.

Our beautiful cottage had successfully survived over 350 years in remarkably good condition only to finally be vanquished by successive destructive storms arriving one after the other in a single final tempestuous winter period. She had tried valiantly to hold herself together to protect the family living within her but the burden had proved too much. Waiting until everyone was safely out she had surrendered her heavy load and crumpled to her knees in defeat.

Several hours later, following a fair bit of time on Google, a quick call to a friend at the Environment Agency for specific local storm data to back up my arguments, a really close re-read of the insurance policy document and some extremely furious typing (that keyboard will never be the same again) and finally my treatise was ready, attached to an email and sent, followed by a paper copy via snail-mail.

A baby step really, but in view of how little progress we had made so far it was a very triumphant baby step indeed.

(Cue: flourishing trumpet fanfare, or maybe not!)

* * *

No response.

Not a dicky bird!

No acknowledgement, no receipt, nothing.

After two days I telephoned the insurance company only to be told that all correspondence, including incoming emails and letters, goes via a department in another county entirely to be scanned before being distributed and that this could take up to a week.

Seriously?

I do realise that the lady on the phone had no idea what our living circumstances were and was not personally responsible for our situation, but the complete lack of concern was a bit much. I was fast running out of the ability to be reasonable.

In the meantime electrical storms were repeatedly battering the English countryside and us.

As I mentioned before, we were aware that electrical storms were quite risky and to lessen that risk we didn't use any electrical equipment while the storms were in progress.

Just as we were getting used to sleeping in a cosy, warm huddle by the fire for the fourth night in a row, an interesting new development occurred. All of a sudden there was an almighty flash of light followed by what sounded like a firework going off inside the front abandoned section of the house. The Barbarians were actually managing to sleep through this but Beloved Husband and I were definitely not so we decided to investigate.

During the previous four nights the storms had resulted in vast quantities of water pouring through the cavernous holes in the broken walls causing lots of water damage. You would be forgiven for wondering why on earth, had we not attempted to cover them with something but you must understand that this was a catch 22 situation. If we did anything at all then we risked the insurance telling us we had made the situation worse by our actions and refusing to help us.

Admittedly they were already refusing to help us, but there was still a remote chance that we might be able to persuade them to reconsider. Therefore apart from some polythene sheeting and a few sand bags to limit how far into the ground floor the incoming rainwater could flow we had not touched the cracks at all. After all we had been strongly advised to stay away from them by the insurance company's own operative.

Anyway the situation that faced us that night was the fact that every flare of lightning generated a surge within the electrical wires in the damaged walls of the cottage and a blaze of sparks would burst out and fly right across the room. Beloved Husband and I hastened to turn the electrics to the entire cottage off at the mains and retreated to a safe distance to watch carefully for the rest of the night with several fire extinguishers handy. Heaven help us if the sparks took hold in the thatch!

I believe that this was the final straw for Beloved Husband, who is usually the soul of reason, diplomacy and discretion.

Not this time, the blue touch paper had been lit and it would be prudent for all to stand well back.

He and I were both done with hopeless despair and self-recrimination.

We had also done rather a lot of polite yet patient exasperation.

In an extremely short space of time we skipped mild irritation, hopped over progressive annoyance, fast-forwarded through extreme aggravation to arrive at complete and utter raging-inferno outrage.

Enough was enough!

Shoving the cat off the lap-top, what followed (at six o'clock that morning, i.e. as soon as we were able to safely turn the power back on of course) was a terse email to the effect that our house was falling down!

They (our insurance company) were refusing to acknowledge their responsibilities. Under the current circumstances there was a very great likelihood that someone might be killed or seriously injured if the property fell any further and in our opinion they were absolutely and completely in breach of their duty of care to us, their customer.

We also drew their attention to the fact that the front wall of the house, which was definitely still moving, would probably sever the oil line to the boiler, which ran at its base, should it succumb to the influence of gravity entirely. This might not only generate an environmental disaster of a significant scale, it would also probably bring the mains electric power and telephone lines to the house down at the same time with potentially unthinkable consequences. We suggested that they might like to consider communication with us with regard to these matters.

We finished our email with the promise that if we had received no response from them by noon that day we would be taking legal action and going to the press. Attached to the email was another copy of my treatise rejecting the original decision and explaining why. This was sent to every single email address we could find on the insurance company's various letters and documents, including those located on the company's website, from local offices to regional, all the way up the ladder to head office.

They couldn't all go to somewhere else for scanning surely?

Obviously not! At precisely one minute past nine that morning the telephone rang.

16: <u>Storm Damage</u>

Definition: damage to a property caused by violent winds, usually in conjunction with rain, hail or snow.

Staying in the past....

Let's take the positives where we can find them.

The news was good, not brilliant, but it was still good. The door that had previously been slammed forcibly in our faces had been re-opened just a teeny, tiny crack. Our caller, who identified himself as someone really incredibly important from somewhere unbelievably, exceedingly lofty, politely accepted that while we were in a very difficult situation, he did not necessarily agree with our opinion that Loss Adjuster Number 1 might have either made an error in judgement or could potentially have been misinformed.

Nevertheless he did concur that perhaps the situation might require a minor review in order to satisfy both parties that no misunderstanding had occurred.

Might we be free perchance on Friday at 10am for a meeting on site to discuss the issue?

Well we certainly had nowhere else more pressing that we needed to be.

A swift confirmatory email followed, outlining that a Professional Gentleman would be attending a meeting at our property all the way from Birmingham. Loss Adjusters Numbers 1 and 2 would also be joining us. Very interesting! Amazing in fact!! How very keen they were to communicate with us all of a sudden. I felt it was a shame that we had to resort to threats to get their attention. Rather sends the wrong message doesn't it? However, needs must!

Given the sheer number of people coming from the insurance company we decided that there would be a degree of safety in numbers and invited our Friendly Local Builder and the knowledgeable Master Roofer along to ensure that any technical talk did not go completely over our heads. The last thing we needed was to be blinded with building science and lose this opportunity to be taken seriously.

The Barbarians were all keen to observe proceedings too and were most helpful over the next few days as we attempted to generate enough space in the kitchen, lounge area and conservatory to put up the dining table and locate enough chairs for the forthcoming meeting. We worked very hard to make the useable part of the house look as clean and tidy as possible despite the fact that it was stacked to the rafters with all our displaced worldly goods.

As the day dawned, having been persuaded by their father as Commander in Chief that they must remain silent while the meeting was in progress, the Barbarians arranged themselves in their pre-agreed battle formation.

Logic had opted to be in charge of hospitality and positioned herself on a stool in the kitchen so that she could discretely produce tea, coffee and biscuits for all present should the opportunity arise.

Due to her on-going mobility issues the Princess of Chaos settled herself on the sofa by the fireplace with her I-pad primed, ready to look up anything technical. She was close enough to hear everything said and had an excellent view of proceedings.

The boys opted for an external surveillance operation and carefully selected two lookout positions up oak trees that provided good visibility of either the front or the back of the property.

Together they formed our very own personal reconnaissance team. Quiet was armed with his I-pod and Small had an ancient walkie-talkie so they could maintain communication with us should it prove necessary.

Beloved Husband and I simply walked up and down the driveway, unable to settle anywhere we were in such a state of anxiety and anticipation. Eventually we huddled like penguins near the gate, for comfort rather than warmth. Beloved Husband repeatedly removed my fingers from my mouth to stop me chomping on my nails with the stress and I kept stuffing them right back in until he wrapped both of his arms around me and held me so tight that I couldn't move at all.

***

Loss Adjuster Number 1 was the first to arrive with another dramatic spray of pea shingle. We were gratified to notice that he removed his entire body from the car, including both feet, which we felt was a promising indication that he intended to stay for longer than two minutes this time.

Having greeted him politely we found we had very little to say, so we waited in awkward silence until the Professional

Accidental Damage

Gentleman from Birmingham arrived with another gentleman who he introduced as Loss Adjuster Number 2. Both of these new arrivals were dressed in very smart pinstripe suits and looked incredibly business like and, well, professional. These gentlemen looked like they made important decisions. We rather felt that our situation warranted an important decision so hopefully they were in the right place and would make the right decision.

They shook hands politely with us and then asked if they could inspect the property. It was made respectfully clear to us that they would come and find us when they wanted to talk to us.

We had been effectively dismissed, in a charmingly inoffensive manner (it takes quite some skill to do that), from our own driveway. We were still mildly miffed though, but dutifully complied, retreating to the conservatory to deploy our secret weapons. Our lookouts were going to come in useful!

We realised at that point that we had made a school boy error. Literally! We had put the wrong school boy in the lookout for the front of the property. Quiet was his usual uncommunicative self in spite of the critical nature of the situation. His habit of sending single word (in some cases single letter) text messages was infuriatingly obscure. After several indecipherable messages I snatched Logic's I-pod and typed 'more words needed, in English, or NO FOOD ever again!'

There was a short silence followed by:
'K'

'I MEAN IT!!!'

'OK. Cool tape measures'

'What?'

'Dad would appreciate their tape measures.'

'?????'

'They have really cool tape measures. Electric. '

'OK I GET THAT BUT FOCUS, WHAT ARE THEY MEASURING WITH THEIR REALLY COOL TAPE MEASURES?' (Yes, it was all in caps, can you tell I was cross?)

'The house,' came the reply.

'DID I MENTION THERE WOULD BE NO FOOD?' I said.

'No. I am serious. They are measuring the house, all of it. The outside, really, really thoroughly,' he said.

That was interesting! I wondered why.

'And they seem to be arguing.'

Even more interesting!

'The man that arrived first was waving his arms around a lot and then he left.'

We had no idea what to make of that, but it sounded like Loss Adjuster Number 1 was now out of the picture.

Accidental Damage

I can't pretend I was terribly sorry about that. I don't think you can really laugh at someone while you are destroying their whole world and then expect them to like you can you? Not that I am one to hold a grudge, he was only doing his job. Maybe he hadn't intended to laugh, perhaps it was a nervous reaction, but I could have done without it.

There followed a message from Small who was engaged in surveillance of the back of the property, letting us know that the other two men were approaching the back of the house.

We braced ourselves.

***

Beloved Husband and I were gratified to note that both Friendly Local Builder and Master Roofer had put in an appearance for the meeting as well, in order to sit very firmly on our team at this critical event. It is at times like these that one is surprised and eternally grateful for the kindness of strangers. Both were busy men and could easily have left us to sink or swim on our own, yet with no guarantee of recompense for their time, they were here standing up for what they felt was right.

I am not totally naïve either though, one wanted to defend his workmanship, the other was quite keen on the contract for the repair but that didn't matter, neither of them, was being deceitful in any way. The fact remained that they were here supporting us and our family. When you are the underdog you take any help you are offered and you are very, very grateful.

After a certain amount of shuffling and shifting of chairs, eventually all persons present were established in a suitable seat around the table in the conservatory with the hot drink of their choice. Believe me it was important that everyone was comfortable because this was going to be a very long meeting. The boys had extracted themselves from their eyries and followed the two men in (after all there was food available) and after quietly ransacking the biscuit tins they settled themselves in the lounge area with their sister, well within ear and eye shot to watch as events unfolded.

There was a moment of tense silence as we all regarded each other.

The Professional Gentleman took a thoughtful sip of tea before opening proceedings. He leaned forward, looked at both Beloved Husband and I one at a time and then said most earnestly "May I say, personally, how sorry I am at what has happened to your lovely home. It must be very difficult for you under the present circumstances."

Well! You could have knocked me down with a feather! There must have been a mistake! Surely they wouldn't have sent us a real-life-human-being?

What a sad state of events had led us to that point. I had honestly not been expecting genuine compassion!

We were braced for sweeping denials of liability, mountains of legalese, and ultimately an outright dismissal of our claim. This kind man could not have made a more effective opening statement. Immediately any defensive feelings of outrage, resentment and hostility that we held towards the unfeeling, faceless company were totally demolished.

Accidental Damage

Empathy aside though, let's not forget that he was here to do a job and we were still in trouble.

As the meeting progressed it became evident that we were dealing with a number of rather tenuous and undefined elements. I must ask you to bear with me at this point as I try and explain. Please remember that the following paragraphs are a note of how I understood the discussions that took place during that meeting. I may not have been entirely correct in my comprehension as it was a very complicated situation.

Primarily the insurance company had yet to determine whether our assessment of storm damage was accurate. It was suggested vaguely that this would require a number of independent assessments to be carried out by specialists. Whilst they stood by Structural Engineer Man's original report, they did agree that, under the circumstances, an assessment by an independent structural engineer, this time one who was definitely an old buildings expert, was required.

This would need to be followed by an assessment to determine whether any of the recent works carried out on the cottage could have been responsible for the collapse (i.e. had any of the work we had had done over the years we had lived there caused the problem). Then dependent on the conclusions of these studies, the insurance company would make a decision as to what degree of responsibility may or may not be held by themselves, with regard to our claim.

That seemed fair enough to us.

Then we came to the reason that required such careful measuring of the property with those impressive tape measures. This was all to do with the rebuild amount stated in our policy documents.

Please understand that I struggled to follow a lot of what was said here but it would appear that we did not have a sufficient rebuild amount stated in the insurance policy documents for the whole property to be rebuilt. Even though we were only looking at a partial repair, apparently they do the maths from your total rebuild insurance figure, working out some relative proportional amount for a partial repair and then decide if you have enough cover. (Yet another minor detail not mentioned when I took out the policy.)

Generally most people establish this figure over the phone just as I had done when inquiring about insurance. I hadn't realised how important this figure would be when it actually came to a claim.

This was going to be a big problem for us as it was the old section of our house that was in trouble and older properties cost so much more to rebuild, putting a disproportionally large figure on a potential partial rebuild or repair. You could happily build a much bigger property, from scratch on the site using modern materials, from the figure quoted so I felt that we could reasonably have expected to be covered. But it doesn't work like that. The existing property was not modern and therefore this insured rebuild sum was not enough. (There's always a slight snag isn't there?)

Accidental Damage

Another major problem was that in the event that they decided that we were covered, any help they might consider giving to us could only ever amount to a 'like for like' compensation, which was in fact a virtual impossibility as they could not give us back a historic, old building. No matter how hard they tried.

They were not allowed to give us anything that amounted to a material gain, and modern building methods and materials constituted exactly that. As our cottage was not a listed building and therefore was not exempt from building regulations, we would have no choice but to comply with modern building standards, the associated value of which, the insurance company were implying, we were not entitled to as they would constitute a distinct material gain. (Hmm, rock versus hard place!)

The silly thing with all this was that while building in modern materials would be faster and more economical than trying to rebuild in cob, nevertheless in terms of pure value the repaired building had the potential to be ultimately worth more in modern materials.

(Confused? Me too!)

Basically, if independent assessments agreed that we were looking at storm damage, and that was a very big 'IF', then they would only able to possibly consider authorising putting us back where we were, originally.

That would be absolutely fine with us, but unfortunately putting us back where we were, was a technical impossibility.

Everything was still very much under dispute. Given the massive costs involved I am not really surprised. I had no idea that these things were so complicated.

So all in all we were not really very much further forward, but at least they were communicating with us and considering authorising (and paying for) the necessary reports. This was relatively good news, but you could be forgiven for thinking that I had started to buy into Beloved Husband's glass-half-empty persona by the sluggish way I was responding. Having had so little sleep in recent weeks, I was incredibly tired and found following the proceedings extremely hard. The truth of the matter was that a large elephant could have jumped up and started tap dancing while simultaneously playing the trombone at that point and I would have struggled to formulate an appropriate response.

Not so the Barbarians. It was evident from the pointed looks passing between them that they were monitoring everything and commenting to each other via their electronic devices. Small had shuffled right up to Chaos and they were muttering to each other as she no doubt explained what was going on to him.

In the meantime however, back with the adults at the table, the fact remained that it would be quite some time before a decision could be reached.

Nevertheless the Professional Gentleman accepted that we were in an untenable position with regard to the continuity of our family life. The tent, the mud, the scattered piles of belongings and the huge holes in the wall had all been duly noted.

Accidental Damage

While the company was not accepting any liability they were open to the discussion of our needs as a family during the time that the question of liability was being established.

Unfortunately, after much discussion the general consensus was that there were very few options for alternative accommodation available locally in which to re-establish our family life at another location. By this I basically understood that hotels and rented houses were off the cards due mainly perhaps to the holiday season, but also potentially because of long term costs that might ensue should the company determine that they were not liable to assist us after all.

I noticed at this point rather a lot of twitching coming from our teenage audience and a flurry of muted, electronic 'pings'. I concluded that there was an intense I-pod messaging conversation going on between the Barbarians as the subject of accommodation was being discussed. Then I realised that Logic was trying to gain my attention.

Employing the rather basic British sign language skills she had acquired whilst helping out at the after school club that term, she was frantically trying to communicate with me. Having only a very rudimentary knowledge myself, I was finding it hard to understand her. I kept thinking she was saying "Remember Cornwall" but couldn't for the life of me think what she might mean.

Eventually, raising her eyes to heaven (teens do that so well, there must be an A-level in it?), she squeezed past the table, marched over to the sofa, grabbed the I-pad off her sister and shoved it pointedly under my nose before sweetly asking the visitors if they would like refills for their hot drinks.

While additional hospitality requirements were being met I quickly glanced at the website on the I-pad screen and instantly comprehended what the girls were suggesting. Nudging Beloved Husband I showed him, and had the satisfaction of watching enlightenment dawn there too.

Our eyes met with suppressed hope.

Such a simple solution.

If only we could get our kind visitors to play ball.

"How would you feel about a static caravan?" inquired my Beloved Husband after clearing his throat. "It would enable the family to stay together on site, protecting the remaining cottage area, prevent any danger of burglary or squatting and facilitate supervision of any repair works that might or might not be agreed." (Two could play at the non-specifics game.)

The Professional Gentleman looked at Loss Adjuster Number 2 and a discrete nod passed between them.

Just like that!

It was agreed that the House Insurance Company would consider covering a one-off cost to buy and site a static caravan in our garden while the liability question of our claim could be more formally established.

Accidental Damage

Beloved Husband was to visit such a caravan emporium later that day to identify an appropriate vehicle and discern costs for purchase, siting and installation. This would be communicated back to the company in writing and if the costs were agreeable then a cheque would be forthcoming to cover it. In the meantime the Professional Gentleman also agreed that the insurance company would cover the costs of the independent reports required to establish ultimate liability on our overall claim.

It would appear that, even though no final decision had been made, we might have reached a temporary compromise.

Regardless of the final outcome of the claim, I do not believe the Professional Gentlemen will ever fully appreciate just what he did for our little family that day.

PART 4

There are dark shadows on the earth, but
its lights are stronger in the contrast

Charles Dickens

17: <u>Salvation</u>

Definition: Preservation or deliverance from destruction, difficulty or evil.

Back in the present day....

It was during that period of time when I was splattering acrylics left, right and centre in my little artist's cubby two years later that I began to realise that perhaps all wasn't as black and white as I had subconsciously painted it.

Admittedly I had made a disastrous mistake, but to be completely fair it could also be suggested that perhaps the house insurance's initial response to us was a genuine error too, not a malicious attempt to wriggle out of their responsibilities. After all once we had eventually managed to get someone to listen to us it became obvious that this was much more of a 'shades of grey' type of situation. (No! Not that sort of shades of grey! Behave!!)

350 year old houses generally don't collapse every day, or no one would ever buy one. (I must confess here that I certainly won't ever buy one again!) I am sure people can't possibly put themselves in this sort of situation for fun. Although, come to think of it, there are some very odd people around.

Thinking back I remembered the additional pressure of knowing that we only had two more weeks left to the school holidays. Crunch time was coming. Without a significant improvement on our current tented accommodation, Beloved Husband and I were genuinely going to have to start making arrangements for the disintegration and dispersal of our beloved Barbarian band around the countryside to live with relatives in proper houses before the school term started, with no real knowledge of when we might be able to bring them home again.

Prior to that first big meeting at the house, I realised that Beloved Husband and I had been totally in the dark about the right way to move forward. It is important to acknowledge that after that point in time we were no longer trying to work out a solution to the overwhelming dilemma before us, on our own.

The situation in which we found ourselves was vastly more complicated than we could ever have imagined but at least there were now other people wrestling with the conundrum too, and they were not unsympathetic to our circumstances even if they didn't yet know how things were going to play out either.

That one critical decision on the part of the Professional Gentleman to offer us a helping hand in the form of more acceptable accommodation, actually on-site at our beleaguered home, was of paramount importance because it gave us time.

As long as we could stay together as a family unit we could figure out the rest.

***

Up until now I seem to have been yacking on a bit about how that whole awful event was affecting me.

I do apologise! So selfish!

Accidental Damage

You could be forgiven for thinking that I wasn't too bothered about how it was affecting my Barbarians. Nothing could be further from the truth. On the whole they gave every appearance of having the time of their lives. As I mentioned previously, it was the school holidays and the lack of any formal routine meant they were in heaven, late nights, non-stop snacks, energetic games followed by uninterrupted, nag free, teen-slobbing time.

One could say that undergoing extremely high pressure events can be character building but I think you would get short shrift from my Barbarians if you dared to mention that. I believe they would comment that their characters had been sufficiently developed for the time being thank you very much, and chilling out was definitely on the cards.

Nevertheless Beloved Husband and I did notice there were a lot more quick hugs flying around though. I don't mean that they were hugging each other you understand, don't be ridiculous! They had the normal, healthy antipathy most siblings have for close proximity to, or physical contact with, each other.

You know the kind of thing I am on about. It generally works along the lines of 'that's my sibling, I can be rude to him/her and act like I hate him/her but you're not family so you can't!' (It works for cousins too!)

So no, don't worry, things were not so bad that the Barbarians were actually going around indulging in group hugs. Nevertheless they were behaving in an unusually polite and civilised manner towards each other and the number of times I would have to step in and mediate had diminished to zero which would have been astonishing had I the wit to notice. On the other hand they were flinging rather a lot of hugs in my general direction which was rather gratifying. Even Quiet, who, as with speech, generally doesn't do physical contact either, would sidle up to me from time to time and give me an awkward one-armed squeeze to the shoulders. That *seriously* never ever happens.

Initially I thought that this was an indicator of how stressed they all were and so kept repeating my rather fraudulent mantra to them that everything would be alright. Looking back though I think it was rather more of an indicator of how stressed they realised that I was and it was their way of demonstrating support and attempting to prop us up.

These Barbarians of ours and their hugs were helping us to hold on when there was genuinely nothing left in us.

18: <u>Reclamation</u>

Definition: the process of taking something back, or reasserting a claim or a right.

Returning to the past...

Static caravans come in all shapes and sizes as we were to learn, and moving them around the country in order to site them involves a whole host of fun and games.

Up until that point in time, two and a half years ago, the presence of static caravans on the road represented a total nuisance to me, causing disrupted traffic flow and delayed journeys. Now, however, I feel rather differently when I see one. Although the majority are probably being relocated for enjoyable purposes such as holiday homes for example, I cannot help but wonder if in fact the caravan being transported is going to save someone from rather more desperate circumstances, as ours was when it finally arrived outside our house on a humungous flat-bed lorry, blocking the country lane entirely for quite a lengthy period.

The gentlemen delivering it looked exhausted as they pulled up and looking at the size of their load I couldn't help marvel. How on earth they had got it through the ford down the road, around the sharp, wiggly bends or even under all the low hanging trees? This latter issue might well have been solved by the young man sat astride the roof of the caravan with a hacksaw.

Obviously the health and safety elf was on holiday that day (it was August after all) and as the day progressed it really became just as well he was.

I had visions of lopped off tree branches being discarded all along their route. The local estate manager was not going to be pleased, but perhaps he wouldn't realise it was us.

Then we came to the rather problematic issue of actually siting our new accommodation in the grounds of our property. When it came down to it we had several basic engineering issues before us. Not least of which was the fact that in order to site the caravan we were going to have to remove the props holding up the wonky, wobbly walls and pass it right alongside them.

Ooops!

Risky?

Just a bit!

The only safe space on the property that was big enough for the caravan to be parked long term was in the back garden and the only route to that space was the opening between the cottage and the garage, an area that was currently stuffed full of supportive metal scaffolding poles.

Added to that, during the manoeuvre there would be only a maximum distance of one inch to spare on either side of the caravan as it passed through the gap meaning that extreme precision was essential. To assist the move, all guttering and external fittings had to be removed from both the side and roof of the garage and the caravan itself, before we even started, and a large section of our front hedge needed to disappear. (Cue our new friend with his handy hacksaw.)

Accidental Damage

Finally, as if we didn't have enough to contend with, should the worst happen and the walls actually fall onto the caravan (and hopefully not any people) then we would have to contend with the mains electricity wire also plummeting earthwards and all the associated mayhem that might ensue. Heck!

Fortunately our team of lorry driver delivery men were definitely not a bunch of faint hearted wimps. They were bred from the type of toughies who eat ten shredded wheat for breakfast followed by a Full English and a cup of tea strong enough to stand a spoon up.

These tall, muscular, confident chaps were not going to let a little thing like potential death and destruction stop them from siting this caravan successfully in spite of the obstacles in their way.

Unfortunately leaving the caravan in the road for the next indefinable period of time and living in it there simply wasn't an option, as demonstrated by the significant tail back of cars that was building up. It just goes to show that even though there are very few houses along this little lane, lots of people use it as a rat run to avoid traffic on the main thoroughfares.

The other interesting thing was that the colourfully expressive language the thwarted drivers were using, when they got out of their cars to remonstrate with our lovely lorry driver about the blocking of the road, tailed off very quickly when they realised the sheer extent of the experimental engineering that was actually in progress. Very few drivers got back in their cars to turn around and find an alternative route. Most stuck around to watch the novelty unfold and some even pitched in to help. A wealth of community spirit was propagated amongst complete strangers who all inevitably had their ten pennyworth of advice to toss in to the mix.

We British do love a good crisis don't we?

So down came the props and the caravan was slowly and painfully inched through the gap with everyone watching the weak and wonky walls with bated breath for the slightest sign of movement. Given our luck so far that summer I didn't have high hopes, but was grateful to be proved wrong as eventually our new accommodation was coaxed into place with no casualties, other than my Beloved Husband's cherished hedge. (What is it with men and hedges?)

A round of applause rose from our audience with much cheering, shaking of hands and clapping of each other on the back.

Perhaps we missed a trick here and should have sent the Barbarians around with an upturned hat for contributions towards the missing £200,000. Had we realised in advance that our little crisis was going to attract such a crowd of on-lookers we could have sold tickets or at least put out some tables and chairs and flogged extortionately priced cream teas. Failing that an impromptu car boot sale on the drive might have cleared some of our remaining junk at least.

It's amazing what could have been achieved with a little hindsight.

Eventually, though, after re-establishing the wibbly, wobbly wall support system with relief and then re-attaching all the fittings removed from the caravan and garage, our new friends the lorry drivers and the young man with the handy hack-saw departed, allowing our captive audience to melt away too and we were left to investigate our new home in peace.

19: <u>Comfort</u>

Definition: The easing or erasing of a person's feelings of pain or upset.

Back in the here and now....

It was at that juncture, painting away in the present, briefly emerging from my entrancement with my recollections of the past, that I realised my artwork was definitely starting to look brighter. The distinctly disturbing demonic edge to my paintings was easing, and with my co-operation, might successfully be urged to depart on a more permanent basis.

Studying my most recently finished piece I could see an underwater scene looking up from the depths of the sea. Oil paint in dark blues and greens at the edges of the canvas blended inwards to lighter turquoise, pale blues and white at the centre. The main feature of this painting was a shoal of silvered fish spiralling in and up towards the light filtering in from the surface of the water. An altogether more positive image I felt. Progress!

After all we cannot wallow in self-pity forever can we? It doesn't half get boring after a while, and I did think I was beginning to feel a bit better about the whole fiasco. The radio on the windowsill was playing a track about wounds healing and the need to forgive oneself. I was beginning to think that this was a jolly good point. We should give ourselves a break from time to time and not be so harsh with ourselves. We are only human after all and life is scattered with potential pot holes to trip us up, no matter how careful we are.

Accidental Damage

Thus, after chomping my way through the sizeable piece of chocolate fridge cake that had magically appeared on my desk with the omnipresent cup of tea, I made an important decision. If my little painted fish could swim towards the light then so could I.

There had been enough self-indulgent scourging over past events. What was done was done. I had faced my demons and acknowledged my crime. It was time to move forward. The prevalence of dark dismal shades in my work should be encouraged to give way to a sunnier and altogether more hopeful parade of happier hues. Moving the still-wet canvas from the easel to the mantel piece, from which vantage point, the little silvery fish could inspire me while the oil dried, I got stuck in sorting out my work space.

Soon a not insignificant stack of murky canvasses lurked out of sight behind me, banished along with my tubes of matt black, burnt umber and Prussian blue. Ahead of me sat a whole pile of bright, white sheets of thick paper, hopefully awaiting the studious application of the remainder of the rainbow.

Starting as I meant to go on I selected a tube of exceptionally cheerful cadmium yellow and let my mind drift back to the early days with the static caravan....

***

It was around about the time of our new mobile home's arrival two years previously, that I became aware of a rather unusual phenomenon. Somehow small plates of edible comfort were appearing at regular intervals in my general vicinity. This started with things like the aforementioned chocolate chip cookies, and the repertoire expanded over time to include chocolate fridge cake, chocolate crispy cakes, chocolate fudge cake and more.

Note if you will the preponderance of chocolate, but please understand that this was balanced out with regular offerings of fruit too. There could be only one or two culprits. It would appear that certain people felt I needed feeding up.

Now it is very true to say that I started this whole debacle in a far more (How shall I put it?) well-upholstered-condition, which was probably a good thing as my appetite was one of the first things to desert me along with the stability of my habitation. (Followed almost immediately by my sound mind, which beat a hasty retreat flapping both arms and screaming loudly!)

As I was in a general state of perpetual stress I had been burning through my carefully laid down stores of fat at a remarkable rate of knots. Whilst not exactly enormous to begin with, (I prefer the term 'comfortably rounded,') I had quickly started to look rather scrawny over the ensuing weeks, which is really a very unfortunate look on me. How do all these models do it? They look slim, energetic, and youthful, radiating supreme health whilst at the same time being stick thin. Whereas, the skinnier version of me simply looked old, tired, haggard and very much in need of being put to sleep sometime very soon. (Hopefully permanently, only joking, I think.)

My darling daughters had obviously decided between them that I needed fattening up and the result was that they were cooking up suitably fat-store-inducing recipes (quite literally!). As the Princess of Chaos was still finding being on her feet for any length of time rather tiring, she formed the research part of the catering team and was responsible for looking up suitably comforting and calorific recipes on line, whilst Logic accomplished the development role by whipping up delicious treats in my fortuitously still fully functional kitchen. Then small bite sized portions were being left in suitably convenient locations in my general vicinity in the hope that I would absentmindedly notice them, gobble them up and instantaneously ingest over 1000 calories in one fell swoop.

Yum, I liked this theory. What intelligent daughters I have. The presence of comfort food on tap with virtually no effort involved on my part was definitely a dream come true for me. Add to that the fact that I had the convenient excuse that I was 'far too thin' and 'needed to eat'. Never in all my born days had I ever heard those phrases applied to me before and probably won't again. Yet it was true, I needed the energy to keep going, so each delicious mouthful was consumed gratefully and held no guilt whatsoever.

There were several other rather lucky knock on effects from all this baking too. Ultimately Chaos and Logic were actually learning to work very effectively together in their little enterprise, and extremely chilled out they were too. After all who doesn't find baking relaxing? In addition to this, they had the boy Barbarians totally in their thrall with this ready supply of previously unheard of sophisticated delicacies requiring conveniently available stomachs, so their co-operation on many less exciting, more physical jobs was guaranteed.

Another positive side effect was that when they ran out of ingredients, Chaos worked out how to set up an online shopping delivery for more and thoughtfully included a basic food, veg and essentials content too. After all if the poor delivery driver was going to have to trek all the way out to the middle of nowhere to find us, he might as well bring us shed-loads of milk and bog roll too. This, happily, meant that I could be relieved of my more arduous supermarket sweep duties and was therefore able to concentrate on more immediate home-salvaging tasks.

As they say necessity is the mother of invention. Prior to our little adventure I am not sure that any of them really bothered to think where the family food supply came from.

20: <u>Bedroom</u>

Definition: A room specifically designed and kept for sleeping in.

Scrambling indelicately up into our beautiful, green, static caravan (yes they are quite high off the ground and yes we had forgotten to order a set of appropriate steps, but never mind) we looked around us with reverence.

This was a typical six bed caravan as you would find located on any holiday camp site all over England and Wales. In fact we had stayed in identical ones in Cornwall for several summer holidays over the years, which is what had given the Barbarians the idea for such garden accommodation in the first place.

You would never believe just how excited we were. After weeks of doom, gloom and wet canvas, here was a bit of pure exhilaration.

No more nights in the tent. No more bending double to get under the tent flap, zipping reluctant canvas sheets closed, crawling under damp duvets to wriggle into cold sleeping bags before trying to roll or squirm into place on the mattress, huffing and puffing with exertion.

In fact the tent had been completely removed in order to make room for the caravan. It was now suspended from the rafters of the garage in a vain attempt to dry it out before returning it to its kind owner. The poles and guy ropes had all been accounted for and the mud wiped from the pegs. The only thing bothering me was how to actually get it back into the bag it came in, but that was an issue for another time. There's only so much you can stress about in one go.

No longer would we have to put a huge amount of effort into the action of simply lying down to rest. We could merely walk into a caravan bedroom and flop onto a bed. Yay!

For nearly two months now every night had been preceded with the whole palaver of either, settling into the tent with sufficient warm layers to see us through the night and remembering to have been to the loo, or alternatively hauling mattresses off stacks in the lounge to place them on the floor as we carefully stoked the fire so that it was hot enough to burn for several hours but not spitting dangerous embers out at us while we slept.

Sometimes one night might involve the employment of both options if, once settled in the tent, an electrical storm started up out of the blue, resulting in a hasty and often soggy retreat from the tent to the house. In fact, storms aside, some nights it simply rained so heavily that sleeping in the tent was like trying to sleep under a drum kit whilst it was being played, so the house was often the better option and we would snooze curled up like a litter of puppies before the fire.

No more!

We had been thrown a life belt, or more accurately a life raft. Like the owl and the pussycat we were about to set off in our own beautiful caravan-shaped pea-green boat to destinations unknown. Unlike them we had neither honey nor money, but we did have each other.

Accidental Damage

Now we had safe, warm civilised sleeping accommodation. Who knows perhaps we would even manage to actually get some sleep. Our immediate future was settled. Regardless of the outcome of the claim, I was willing to bet that the insurance company wouldn't whip this caravan away from us while we needed it so desperately. It wouldn't be worth the adverse publicity to them to make a family homeless in these circumstances and I certainly wouldn't have kept quiet about it. It was also a fairly dubious notion that we would ever get it out of the garden again anyway, such a tight squeeze had it been to get it in.

This caravan had all the mod cons, heating (which we were really going to need come winter), electric lighting, running water and more importantly bedrooms! There was a master bedroom right up the far end, for Beloved Husband and I, with a small double bed (emphasis on the 'small' here – it really is just as well we like each other - the sheets from our old bed went around this mattress twice, how cute!) and a dinky little en-suite toilet. It was useful that I had lost that bit of weight I mentioned, because it soon became obvious that only stick insects go to the loo in these caravans. I must admit the term 'master suite' was far too grandiose for the space allocated but we really were not feeling fussy.

Beggars not being choosers and all that!

Next to the master bedroom was the first of two twin rooms which could only be described as extremely snug. (Aren't we lucky that the Barbarians are getting on so well these days?) This twin room was marginally larger than the other and it was decided that the two boys would occupy it for several reasons. Firstly they were the smallest two members of the tribe and thus the obvious contenders for sharing a small twin room. Secondly it was their habit to stay outside playing sport until the very last minute before falling into bed and dropping off to sleep almost as soon as their heads touched the pillow, so really they would spend very little time actually conscious in this tiny room anyway. Hence it was decided that their close proximity to each other wouldn't be too much of a major problem.

The other twin room presented us with a bigger problem though, as it was really very small indeed. One wonders whether it was in fact designed for twin guinea pigs rather than two humans. Nevertheless, as I said before, we were not complaining. We had become the most resourceful of individuals over the previous few weeks and as such immediately put our minds to identifying a suitable answer. Difficult situations really do inspire ingenious solutions.

Thus it was decided that Logic should take ownership of the second twin room as Beloved Husband would drag her own small double mattress from its current position in the stack in the lounge and wedge it into the teeny tiny room on top of the two miniature single beds that were already there thus turning the whole room entirely into one bed. She need simply open the door and hurl herself bodily inwards at bedtime to spend the most comfortable of nights in what was effectively her own cosy little cupboard. (Just like a certain famous young wizard but with nicer family ties.)

Then we had only one more sleeping space to find.

I was keen that the Princess of Chaos should not remain sleeping in the house on her own. We were a team and as such should stick together. Added to that I knew I would only spend a significant amount of time trotting between house and caravan in paranoid circles, to check on her, so from a purely selfish point of view I insisted we find a way to accommodate her in the caravan as well.

It transpired that the caravan also had a dinky little bathroom (small toilet, mini sink and a shower of upright coffin-like proportions) and a kitchen-dining-living area of compact yet functional design. As our own kitchen-dining-living area in the main house was still very much accessible, operational and significantly larger, it was decided that we would continue to use these during the daytime unless it became absolutely necessary to retreat during future building repairs. Any such repairs were way off in the very dim and distant future right at that point so we decided not to worry about them just then. (One thing at a time!)

The single most exciting innovation that the kitchen-dining-living area in the caravan had to offer us was the discovery that the incredibly uncomfortable looking sofa actually pulled out to form a small double bed. It should be noted that the pitifully thin mattress would not be an immense source of great luxury in the longer term, so Beloved Husband applied the same inspiration as before (he was definitely in an impressively inventive mood) and hauled the other small double mattress from the lounge and wedged it on top of the pull out sofa bed.

Thus the Princess of Chaos could rest in regal comfort in this section of the caravan. Once we were all ensconced in our new bedtime locations with the doors shut, all could access bathrooms for night time trips without disturbing each other and so everyone was happy with the new improved sleeping arrangements.

The result was that we all had a hopefully comfortable and relatively private space which belonged to us. Each tiny little room had miniscule wardrobes and or cupboards and we were all keen to commence marking our individual territories like cats, although using boxes of reclaimed belongings rather than actually spraying foul scented substances. (Not so sure about the boys though but I just decided to leave them to it.)

How lovely it would be to be able to hang clothes in wardrobes again, even if the judicious use of a crow bar were needed to get them in and out, so tightly would they be crammed in.

The only remaining issue with the caravan was one of access.

We needed a set of steps. Beloved Husband disappeared off at that point to be original and imaginative in the garage with parts of an old railway sleeper that he had unearthed from a shed at the bottom of the garden during our enforced clear out several weeks earlier. I put the kettle on for a nice cup of tea.

Under normal circumstances my Beloved Husband would be utterly devastated if you dumped a 30 foot mobile home on his beautifully manicured lawns. (Fellas are just as funny about grass as they are hedges in my experience.) However our new arrival, which was immediately christened Hattie by the Barbarians, (No I don't know why, I didn't ask, I was too busy, but everything gets a nickname in this house.) was greeted with open arms and must have triggered Beloved Husband's latent nesting instincts. No sooner had the lorry drivers disappeared over the horizon, there he was making plans to lift up some old broken paving slabs and lay a path, crazy paving style, from the patio to the caravan door complete with flowering pot plants and a two seater bench. (Was it so far from the house to the caravan that he thought we might need a quick sit down on the way? Although on second thoughts, given Chaos' mobility issues this was to prove quite a good idea.)

Then all that was left to do was to finish moving in properly, so we set about once again rearranging boxes and carting belongings around the garden.

21: <u>Gossip</u>

Definition: Casual chatting, generally about other people, usually including details that are not necessarily true.

Back in the future I was going to have to accept the inevitable and stop painting for a while. I had selfishly dabbled away for several days now, and was delighted to see the emergence of more positive pieces. Currently on the easel in front of me was a part-finished acrylic image of a saxophone, all bright, hopeful colours, dancing in the sunlight that was pouring through the window onto the page.

Noting the absence of a comforting titbit and restorative cup of tea at my elbow, I surmised that Logic must be otherwise engaged, no doubt there was some taxing A-level physics conundrum tying up her energies somewhere. While I have no illusion with regard to my own intellectual limitations, all bias aside, I appear to have produced some surprisingly academic offspring. (OK, Beloved Husband did have something to do with it too.)

I supposed I should really re-engage with my beautiful band of Barbarians rather than spend my whole life daubing away at dubious musical instruments.

Still, it was a very nice saxophone!

Nevertheless, while two weeks off work sounded great, it didn't mean two weeks off running this family home, so putting my brushes to one side I thought I had better do a quick Barbarian head count. Chaos was away at university learning about all things highly intelligent so I didn't need to track her down. As predicted Logic was tussling with the mathematical principles of some physics experiment in her room and best left undisturbed. So, after peeping in at her, I set forth to pin down the boys' whereabouts.

Not a difficult task as it happens. I located them easily, in the kitchen. It was obviously Scooby-Snack time because Quiet was energetically engaged in stuffing the entire contents of the fridge into a French stick, (yes a whole one) ably assisted by his sous-chef Small. No doubt the 'snack' would eventually be sawn in half and consumed at lightning speed along with the recently opened family size pack of crisps I spotted by the bread bin. Just as well it is only another hour and a half until tea-time, there was a real danger that they could starve without that little sarnie to keep them going!

Averting my eyes from the scene of devastation (In the interests of full disclosure I should admit that it wasn't exactly tidy before they started.) I decided to leave the discussion about people clearing up after themselves, until later on. I had learned the hard way that coming between a teenage boy and his food was an extremely reckless thing to do. Expecting any sort of a positive response at all to verbal communication was best achieved after nourishment had been consumed and not before. All that sugar in the blood stream having a very useful calming effect on any growling, growing-boy hormones. Choosing which battles to fight had been one of the excellent pieces of parenting advice the A.P.s had given me. (Thanks A.P.s! You're fab!)

Instead I congratulated myself on having two such co-operative young men who obviously enjoyed each other's company, even if the collaboration was more driven by the fact that two of them were able to carry far more food away from the scene of a fridge raid than one, rather than from any real brotherly affection.

So, that was all of my Barbarians' locations effectively established! Jolly successfully too. They were all still alive. Job done!

Carnage in the kitchen aside, I braced myself and ventured bravely towards that space which is grandly referred to by all as the utility room. This is actually little more than a large walk-in cupboard located next to the kitchen which contains a battered old washing machine and the boiler. As I suspected, the laundry pile had been engaged in rapid reproductive activity in recent days and was now starting to overflow the utility room onto the kitchen floor. We were in imminent danger of disappearing under our own dirty washing. (Better than disappearing under someone else's I suppose, but still preferably avoided.) Dragging it all out and roughly sorting it into mountains of lights and darks I shoved the first load into the machine and switched it on.

Then I turned my attention to the dry washing festooned around the conservatory on drying racks. I defy anyone from a large family to say they actually use their conservatory for sitting in. For seventy five percent of the year, ours is definitely engaged in intense laundry related duties only, and as such is always full of washing at various stages of drying. Where else are we supposed to put it when it's either always raining or too cold to dry clothes outside?

The only time our conservatory is free of laundry is if there are visitors coming and I have had sufficient notice to stuff it all out of sight and hide the wire racks so that we can actually get to the wicker chairs in order to plant our bums on them.

While sorting through the dry clothes and allocating them into appropriate piles for each Barbarian I am humming a little tune contentedly.

Well that's a change!

I sound almost happy.

Considering what I have been forcing myself to think about recently I am mildly surprised. Usually such deep reflection leaves me stomping around and snarling for hours. The Barbarians don't have a monopoly on uncivilised behaviour in this household you know. Equal opportunities and all that!

Nevertheless, thinking back, it was true that with the arrival of the wonderful Hattie and the removal of the camping component of our existence, we had moved into a far more stable way of life and a certain degree of contentment was achieved relatively quickly.

We still had no idea how we were going to fix our home, or indeed how long such a thing might take, but the family unit was safe and a form of normality could be resumed.

We were winning.

In the face of seemingly insurmountable odds we were doing alright!

It is not surprising then, when you remember how difficult achieving anything was back then, that nowadays I was quite content folding up the never ending piles of laundry for my Barbarians while appreciating the nice, safe, warm and dry home environment around me with its agreeably sturdy structure.

So content was I, in fact, that I started to remember some of the more entertaining things that had happened back then too. One such occurrence had happened totally out of the blue during a quick trip into the village one day, just after we had finished moving into the caravan.

Now, it should be remembered that we were living in the country where not a lot ever happens. Therefore, as I believe I have mentioned before, anything that does take place locally is always up for grabs entertainment-wise especially when it comes to rumour, gossip and scandal. The best source of such hearsay is always to be found when standing in the queue at the village store. On one particularly hot day when the Barbarians had worked extremely hard moving boxes and furniture around to help me get everything sorted, I had decided to pay the local store a visit for some ice creams and lemonade. A reward for their uncomplaining hard work, if you will!

Standing in the queue and minding my own business (everyone says that but it isn't true) I couldn't help but overhear (they always say that too) what the two rather substantial ladies in front of me were saying in the hushed yet still quite strident tones of the true gossipmonger.

Apparently there were these dreadful incomers (recent arrivals, not true country folk) who had deliberated knocked down their Grade 2 listed (very old and extremely precious) property in order to get around the rigid local planning laws so they could force the planners to grant them permission to build some modern, metal and glass monstrosity.

I tried not to snort at the stupidity of such an action. After all I, myself, as a local, had frequently communicated with the planners with regard to the subtle improvements we had made at our own place and I knew how careful you had to be not to fall foul of the very strict but, on the whole, necessary rules. Intrigued, I shuffled a bit closer in order to hear more. This sounded very juicy indeed.

They say that eavesdroppers never hear any good about themselves and so it proved true as the blabbermouth before me continued with her tittle-tattle, because of course now she was regaling her friend with the fact that these dreadful people had moved lock, stock and barrel into an expensive, luxury hotel and now had the gall to install a huge sixty foot green mobile office in their garden for the workmen! The delivery lorry had blocked the road for two whole days by all accounts.

Would you ever believe it?

No I blinking well wouldn't!

You guessed it, the bloated bigmouth before me was talking about us. Well a fantasy version of us anyway. (Yes, yes alright, what I said was considerably ruder inside my head, but I refuse to be caught swearing in print.)

It was rather regrettable (or alternatively quite fortuitous depending on your point of view) that an extra member of staff opened up an additional till in the shop at that point and the queue was dealt with much faster. As a result I was never to find out what else the old trout had to regale us with, but you could say that I had probably heard enough. Paying for my goods I quickly left the shop and scurried back to my house, the one that I had apparently deliberately and illegally knocked down. How? Seriously I'd love to know!

Well what did you expect? I was hardly going to bash her over the head with a French stick and swear colourfully until the police carted me off to the cells.

For heaven's sake this isn't EastEnders!

In any case, on reflection, I wasn't sure that I didn't prefer her fantastic version of events. In that world it sounded like we had lots of money and got to live in a luxury hotel!

Excellent!

Bring it on, I say!

Chuckling away to myself whilst sorting underpants in my conservatory in the future, it wasn't long before I realised I had run out of washing to fold so I dumped the piles in the appropriate bedrooms in the vain hope that the Barbarians might actually put them away and then moved on to throwing bleach around in the bathroom for a bit. The smell of bleach always gives the illusion that a bathroom has recently been cleaned, even if the opposite is true.

Content that I had at least tried to do a bit of housework I subsequently, gave myself permission to disappear back into my little art room and pick up my paint brushes again.

PART 5

You do not truly know how strong you can be, until being strong is the only option you have left.

Unknown

22: <u>Investigate</u>

Definition: the process of systematically inquiring into facts in order to find out the truth.

So, back to the crumbling cottage once more.....

It was probably fortunate that we had plenty to keep ourselves occupied settling into the caravan as the required surveys of the house that had been requested by the insurance company were going to take some time to organise. We merely got on with establishing our cosy little home environment and the new school term was well under way by the time the next appraisal of the cottage took place, this time by someone who knew rather alot about old cob buildings. Thank goodness.

Early one Monday morning our Genuine Old Building Expert arrived on the property, exactly when he had said he would when he had politely telephoned the Friday before.

An extremely kind and reliable sort of traditional English gentleman, he had a calming and reassuringly trustworthy manner to him and seemed truly distressed to see the state that our poor old cottage was in.

Having now satisfied ourselves that our family was out of the immediate danger of being dispersed to temporary homes around the country, Beloved Husband and I had also had time to ponder the degree of damage done to the cob and to mourn the demise of such a beautiful old building with so much history. The cottage first appeared on maps in the early 1700s and so had been built in the aftermath of the English Civil War. That was a truly long time ago and it would have stood throughout the entire agricultural revolution, the reign of the early Hanoverian kings and Bonnie Prince Charlie landing in Scotland to unsuccessfully re-claim the British throne from them in 1745. The Seven Years war between Britain and France, the outlaw of slavery, the American War of Independence and much, much more, and that's only what happened in the 1700's. Better not to get me started on the rest.

So it's established, even though all those events didn't actually happen right here, this little cottage still represented a significant connection with the past. We felt responsible for it and could not believe it was disintegrating on our watch. Contrary to what the gossiping goon in the village shop had suggested we loved this sweet, old cottage and had very much wanted to live in it. No modern metal monstrosities for us. It was time to find out what sort of repair was potentially possible.

Having spent a very long time examining the cottage in detail, the Genuine Old Buildings Expert consumed several cups of tea and a large slice of chocolate fudge cake before departing laden with copious measurements and information. There wasn't a nook or cranny, from loft to ground floor, that hadn't been thoroughly evaluated. A detailed report would be produced in the coming weeks and we had only to wait for all to be made clear as to why this disaster had befallen our lovely home.

***

So we were left in limbo to wait for the results of the investigation.

In the meantime, there are so many enchanting quirks to life in a caravan that I feel I must share some of them with you here otherwise you will entirely miss the bewitching truth of life on wheels. I know we didn't actually go anywhere in it, Hattie being of the static variety, but this caravan still had teeny tiny wheels and we were definitely on a journey of sorts so I think the analogy applies.

The delightfully early dawn chorus as heard from a caravan was only slightly diminished from that audible in the tent. However in the caravan it was also accompanied by the fascinating addition of a tap dancing element, as the birds scuttled into formation on top of the metal roof above us.

The gentle fall of rain on the caravan roof was rhythmic and soothing. Wait a minute! When do we ever get gentle rain in this country? In truth it was like living under a jack hammer (in use), but modern ear plugs are a marvel, such a wonderful invention.

The charmingly mild rocking action that ensued whenever anyone moved in the caravan was vastly entertaining as long as no one suffered particularly from motion sickness. This movement was significantly enhanced with any sudden action resulting, for example, in all occupants of the caravan being very much aware if any one of the other inhabitants turned over in bed or staggered to the toilet in the middle of the night.

I also found out that yes it was possible to get stuck in the caravan en-suite toilet. I learned the hard way that you had to open the door and reverse in carefully to avoid this scenario as escape proved difficult otherwise. Space was at a premium in that little room, trying to turn around was really not necessary with a little forethought, nor was it very advisable.

Beloved Husband avoided accidentally being entombed in the loo by paying brief nocturnal visits outside as only men can. He was only spooked a couple of times by the horses in the field wandering over to investigate what he was up to.

Caravan living required an extremely petite lifestyle which can mean many advantages to the busy working parent. After all there was so little floor space why on earth would I think to hoover it? And with such tiny rooms the Barbarians couldn't possibly keep them tidy so there was no point in nagging! Plus you always had a ready excuse for being late, scruffy, and tired, not to mention never being able to find anything, so it was an ideal win-win situation.

Furthermore it brought the whole family so much closer together. Quite literally!

One of the beauties of having immensely small bedrooms was that I could hear if the boys were mucking about in the next room and simply had to stick an arm out of bed and knock on the dividing wall, to remind them that there were witnesses within earshot. It worked if they were snoring at night too. In Hattie there was no need to get out of bed and walk down the corridor to go and nudge them to shift into to a less snore-inducing position, a mere hammering of a fist on the wall and the noise would disturb them sufficiently that they grumbled and turned over. (Ok everyone else would grumble too but you can't make an omelette without cracking eggs.)

You have to use the positive where you can find them. You might suggest that were we not in such close proximity I wouldn't hear my boys snoring but I would say that you have no concept of just how loud a Barbarian snore can be. I am deadly serious. My boys could win an Olympic gold medal in snoring. (It is all their dad's fault of course!)

It just goes to show that one can make good use of many situations. We found it was even possible to test Small on his spellings, in the cold early mornings before school, without getting out of bed, simply calling the words through the wall and awaiting the correct sequence of appropriate letters to come back in response.

There were many idiosyncrasies of long term static caravan life too, that had to be experienced to be fully appreciated. For example you might think how useful it was to have a bathroom in the caravan. I will grant you that the toilets were extremely useful, particularly at night, but I would suggest that the term bathroom is far too grand for the stick-insect sized shower facility that actually existed in dear old Hattie.

With even more diminutive dimensions than the tiny en-suite toilet off the main bedroom, the communal shower unit required serious mental athletics before attempting to insert your physical being into its confines. By that I mean it was necessary to decide which part of your body you were attempting to wash before actually getting in and then you had to work out how you were going to achieve it. For example if you wished to wash your hair then you needed to turn on the water before getting into the cubicle with your hands already raised above your head with shampoo at the ready, because once inside there was no chance of actually bending your elbows sufficiently to bring your arms back down to your sides.

Similarly you needed to decide whether you wished to be scalded or frozen during your shower, as at no point was the water ever at a comfortable temperature regardless of how much one fussed with the controls. This initially led to several inventive invectives in the first few early mornings after Hattie's arrival before we all decided to give up on the caravan shower and leg it across the garden into the house to use the bathroom there.

In the general spirit of enhance camaraderie that had sprung up amongst our little band, there were thankfully no arguments over the restrictive bathroom schedule. The Barbarians simply started to check with each other the day before with regard to who was going to shower when and all progressed with surprisingly smooth civility.

Do remember though that when you have rearranged your entire worldly goods under emergency circumstances and then rearranged them all several more times between a variety of ad hock locations including the house, shed, tent, then house again and finally caravan, you cannot ever truly expect to locate things ever again. I guarantee that whatever it was that you wanted would not be in the same place that you ever found yourself searching.

This occasionally proved understandably frustrating if, for example, you needed to leave the caravan during a torrential rainstorm and you realised that all the coats and umbrellas were currently residing quite happily in the house. This factor definitely promoted rather more fore-thought than our previous existence had required so some handy new skills were being learned by all during this period.

The early morning treks through the garden to the house for breakfast were demonstrably refreshing, especially in winter, when a brutal icy blast of morning air proved far more effective at waking you up than splashing cold water on your face from the sink in a nice warm bathroom.

Having to go outside to go to bed in the evening certainly made it easier to remember to complete our primary school aged Barbarian's science homework to chart the waxing and waning of the moon over a three week period. (Yes I admit I am rather grasping at straws here in my attempt to find silver linings.) Nevertheless, the moon was right there in front of us lighting our way, except for when it was cloudy of course, or raining but we couldn't have everything.

Joking aside those evening and early morning walks up and down the garden were actually quite relaxing, when the weather was dry. The fields around the house would frequently be bathed either in moon or dawn light and took on a magical quality, the beauty of which would never be fully appreciated from inside the house.

We were fortunate that the weather was generally kind to us that year and even though there were thunderstorms, we were spared the truly tempestuous downpours of the year before. In contrast the fresh crispness of frosty mornings was quite delightful once you learned to layer up sufficiently prior to sticking your nose out of doors. We invested in some salt to grit the path between Hattie and the house to ensure no slippage during the really icy spells as autumn gave way to true winter.

Accidental Damage

But I am rushing ahead with my story now. We still have the on-going debate about the house repair to discuss. There were yet more investigations to be carried out.

What fun!

***

Several weeks after our encounter with the delightful Genuine Old Buildings Expert we opened our house to yet another independent evaluator. I would like to say we opened our doors to him but he used the hole in the wall like everyone else.

We were going to have to do something about that cavity soon because the weather was definitely closing in and autumn was well established even though it wasn't too wet yet.

You may well ask why we were dawdling, why not shove a whole lot of plywood and polythene over the gap and seal it all up as best we could? Please understand that we really wanted to do this, but due process had to be allowed to take place before any action could be instigated. Had we made any changes at all in the intervening time, other than the necessary propping agreed, then a true evaluation of events could not be carried out and we had been advised that there was a real risk that the insurance company would quite legitimately refuse all liability based on lack of evidence. They were a business after all not a bottomless pit of money (shame!) and therefore needed to justify any release of finance with regard to settlement of claims.

So regardless of how damp and dismal it was living in the remainder of the house during the day with a socking great hole in the wall, we had little choice but to comply. It was only fair to everyone involved to establish the true facts of the matter once and for all. Believe me when I say that such a statement is a lot easier to say with hindsight. At the time, watching my damaged home rot before my eyes, I can assure you that I was not nearly as sanguine about the whole situation.

Fundamentally these two specific evaluations were an essential part of establishing a way forward. The first was to identify conclusively what had caused the collapse and the second was to establish whether any of the building work that we had had done at the house over the years could have been a contributory factor.

These two analyses were as independent as possible. They were paid for by the Insurance Company but they were commissioned on our behalf after a long exhaustive search for appropriately qualified people. Believe me there are not that many people highly experienced in dealing with cob.

It was hoped that the results would fairly ascertain what degree of liability lay where so that a plan to move forward could be formulated to everyone's satisfaction.

It was also to be hoped that the copious cups of tea and enormous slices of cake Chaos, Logic and I were dishing out to all and sundry did not count as bribery.

23:<u>Protective</u>

Definition: guaranteeing preservation from injury or harm

Back in the present...

Later in the evening, my blissful painting experience is rather marred by Logic bustling in. As I return to reality in a somewhat dazed condition, I try to listen carefully as she proceeds to tell me she's off out to a party. It won't be late, she won't be drinking and I can pick her up at midnight.

Oh can I?

Goody!

Also where, when, who with and how?

Only a few of the many questions that immediately spring to mind, followed by "Does your Dad know?"

'Aha!' I hear you say, 'so she is a normal teen after all! In spite of all that useful baking of cakes and making of cups of tea for you. She can still make you suffer like the rest of the population just as a true teenage daughter should!' (I never said she was a saint!)

Even though, of all my Barbarians, this particular one is especially sensible and can be relied upon to be careful, it doesn't reduce the worry potential.

I have learned over the years that there is a very fine line indeed between being a supportive parent and an overprotective, paranoid wreck.

The practical part of me (admittedly this doesn't command an impressively large percentage of my overall make up) believes wholeheartedly in the process of learning from one's mistakes. The paranoid wreck within me just cannot bear yet another trip to casualty so will you please listen to me and stop doing that NOW!!!!

For someone who really hates hospitals the sheer number of trips to medical establishments over nineteen years with four children has resulted in a truly staggering number of hours waited, miles driven, car parking tickets paid for and grey hairs generated. I believe I should be awarded a long service medal, possibly my own hospital car park space or more pertinently my own personal, little, white, straight jacket and a padded cell where I can recover in peace.

Please?

I do recognise that the Paranoid Parent element of my complex personality cannot be allowed full reign, and that on the whole I should just relax and let life happen; enjoying the peace and tranquillity of not worrying about what might go wrong. Nevertheless we should add in my overall luck factor, or rather my lack of luck. Hopefully without indicating an overbearing sense of self-importance, Murphy's Law could have been written just for me.

If it can go wrong, it will.

Butter side down.

Accidental Damage

While other parents are cheerfully enjoying social events, chatting to other happy, relaxed parents, their offspring engage in meaningful but safe activities, I am always the one with a child stuck up a tree and hanging on by their fingertips, or about to throw themselves in a river just for the sheer fun of it. Or, on one memorable occasion, both perilous activities at once! (Excellent multi-tasking skills demonstrated by that particular child.)

Why? It's not fair. If I take my eye off the safety ball you can bet your bottom dollar that casualty is the very next stop for us. (Do not pass GO. Do not collect £200,000.)

Generally at all events requiring a Supportive Parent type there will inevitably be a fair percentage of the Paranoid Parent sort pitching up too. (In my case, I feel that both parental forms arrive within the one body and tussle throughout the event for supreme command.)

For example, with every school rugby match I will dutifully attend dressed in every warm layer I possess and cheer my son on from the side line, yelling loudly "Go on, son TACKLE HIM!!!" along with all the other parents. (After all we want to win don't we?) Nevertheless inside me there will also be a little voice saying "Don't you dare let him stomp your head into the ground again! It'll hurt you fool!" and "How on earth am I going to get all that mud out?" whilst simultaneously calculating the fastest route to the nearest casualty department, just in case.

When my Paranoid Parent personality is in full control, I have been known to go to events with bags of frozen peas packed in cool boxes with ice blocks in the back of my car in anticipation of multiple soft tissue injuries being sustained. I have so frequently been amazed at how long it can take the staff at any sporting facility to produce ice if you need it, especially once you have explained that you don't want it floating around in a large vat of fizzy drink.

On the whole though Supportive Parent generally wins the internal power struggle and at the end of the match I can smile and chat with the other parents as we trot off for a nice thawing cup of caffeine whilst the bedraggled, mud spattered team straggle off to shower, change and demolish twice their body weight in refreshments to replace the energy expended on the pitch.

Back to this instance in particular, though, considering how hard Logic has been working for her A-levels, I realise that she is due a bit of fun. All work and no play and all that! So I decide to let supportive parent win and agreed that she could go to the party, settling in for an evening of hovering by my mobile phone and checking that I still have signal, just in case she needs rescuing and texts me asking for help.

A parent's job is never an easy one!

After all if she never went out we'd be worrying that she was anti-social and didn't have any friends wouldn't we?

24: <u>Stoicism</u>

Definition: the suffering of pain or difficulty without showing feelings or complaining.

Now where was I?

Ah! Yes! Back in the past, we were waiting for the independent assessment reports.

As with all professional reports these took quite some time to materialise, but we were busy enduring our cramped caravan existence and getting on with the business of everyday life, including the school term and our jobs.

Several weeks later two things happened, the October half term arrived and so did the two reports.

The first concluded that which I had suspected, in that the old walls had become damaged by the action of driving rain under the influence of high winds during a series of unusually significant storm events in quick succession. The result being that the footings of the walls had become washed out leaving little or no support for the weight above.

Hence storm damage was officially confirmed as the cause of our wibbly, wobbly walls. So far so good you might say!

The second report concluded that the previous building work at the property had all been carried out in an acceptable manner and therefore did not constitute a contributory factor to the cob collapsing.

Excellent news! You would be forgiven for thinking that all our problems were over, that knights in shining armour would now swoop in and fix our house for us in record time and it would all be over like a bad dream.

If we lived in a Disney movie you would be right, that would probably be precisely what would happen. Sadly no!

That is not how these things work unfortunately.

Nevertheless, you are right this did constitute a big step forward. Through the conclusions of these two reports the cause of the collapse had been irrefutably established and was confirmed in writing in a charming email from Loss Adjuster Number 2.

Accidental Damage was now a thing of the past. A dim and distant memory, thank goodness. However this was only a tiny baby step in the grand scheme of things to come. We had successfully opened a whole new can of worms.

Now that Storm Damage was on the table, it was necessary to establish to what degree our claim might potentially be settled. Apparently, that wasn't going to be straight forward and required yet more reports to be done.

Of course it did!

Great!

Why would we expect anything else? After all there were still more trees left on the planet to cut down to make the paper for these reports, therefore the reports needed to be written. (Sorry I am ranting, I will try to stop that I promise!)

Accidental Damage

There were a number of questions which would need to be answered and another meeting with Loss Adjuster Number 2 was scheduled. This took place at the end of the half term holiday and a number of issues were discussed at length.

I should point out at this juncture that the girl Barbarians still didn't think that their parents could be trusted to handle a meeting with the loss adjuster without them. As a result they had both taken up creative culinary posts in the kitchen from which they could eavesdrop with impunity.

Logic, standing at the breakfast bar, was beating the stuffing out of something white in a clear Pyrex bowl, an icing sugar dust halo hovering gently over her head. Next to her, Chaos had chosen a sophisticated savoury option and was perched on a stool attempting to first blanche and then peel 1000s of cherry tomatoes to make soup.

The boys however had decided their talents were best put to use charging around the garden like maniacs. That left Beloved Husband and I to sit at the dining table in the conservatory with Loss Adjuster Number 2 trying to get our heads around the next stage of the procedure.

As I mentioned before, should a rebuild/repair be authorised, we were only theoretically entitled to 'like for like' in our policy, which in this case would mean re-building in cob and this proved to be the first in a whole series of sticking points that were slowing up the decision making process.

Modern cob building methods are not necessarily the same as ancient cob building methods. I would be surprised if anyone really knew precisely how it was really done hundreds of years ago, but they no doubt have some very interesting theories. Nevertheless whatever cob reconstruction method might be employed it would definitely be fiendishly expensive and the insurance company were understandably not keen on this unless it was absolutely essential, which as the house was not listed it wasn't.

Secondly, to rebuild in cob would take a very long time to accomplish, as work could only take place in the dry months of the year and therefore the rebuild might have to take place over several successive summers. I think you can understand why neither we nor the insurance company were keen on this particular option.

As a result we were immediately moving away from 'like for like' territory which was inevitably going to make things difficult.

It might be thought that as a cob rebuild was so expensive then surely we could simply be allocated that amount of money and spend it how we liked on a general cottage rebuild. Any leftover finances could surely be used for a long foreign holiday in the sun somewhere to get over the shock of it all! (Joke!)

Now I am not the brightest bunny in the hutch but even I knew that wasn't going to happen. (Such a shame! I can't remember the last time I got a tan, and that's got nothing to do with it no longer being considered healthy or trendy.)

Any money released to us for any rebuilding work was going to understandably need to be fully justified and the work would need to be confirmed as having been completed appropriately by an independent third party. This would protect all involved and should ensure that any repairs were carried out to an appropriately professional level and the insurance company could then be confident in continuing to insure the building into the future.

Putting a cob rebuild aside, modern building methods now needed to be considered. Not surprisingly we had rather gone off the quaintness of cob over the last few months and were quite keen on a bit of concrete.

These modern methods had the advantage of being considerably cheaper and faster but the disadvantage was they would potentially result in greater overall value being added to the finished building which couldn't be permitted under the terms of the insurance policy. Thus we have sticking point number 3.

I should explain why Beloved Husband and I were feeling quite so very jaded at this particular meeting, especially as it was really not helping our general comprehension of the complicated proceedings.

You might think that this weary outlook was purely due to the whole falling down house stress and living in a caravan in the garden issue. You would be right to a point, but what you don't know is that we had foolishly added to our sleep deprivation problems recently by agreeing that the kids could have a Halloween party two days before. After all what better setting than a real-life, ancient, falling down, wonky house for that extra spooky feel?

Given the state of the place, we didn't even really have to make any additional Halloween decorations, but that didn't stop us. My particular favourite was the scarily realistic, life-sized skeleton covered in fake gore that Beloved Husband had left slumped right up against the old cottage door. (Don't ask me where he got it from. I really don't want to know.)

In fact Skelly, as he was immediately christened, was so effective that we decided to keep him long after Halloween was over. He proved a great deterrent to discourage people from ducking under the lines of red warning tape around the house and trespassing too close to the wobbly walls.

Beloved Husband had a habit of moving him periodically, purely for his own amusement. I would frequently come home from work to find Skelly engaged in any number of activities from dangling half out of one of the holes in the wall, doing chin-ups from an upstairs window ledge, or apparently climbing through the crack between the wall and the roof waving maniacally. I was relieved to see that his sense of humour hadn't completely deserted him, and the Barbarians found it hilarious.

It should be remembered that there was absolutely no electricity available to the front of the house at all, due to the damage, and no street lighting either, due to the deepest darkest country location. Fortunately, for the party Halloween fell on an eerily clear moonlight night that showed the damaged walls off extremely effectively with the help of a few pumpkin lanterns littered around the place. Possibly a bit too effectively, if I am completely honest, as almost all parents refused to let their kids get out of the car until they had rung us on their mobiles to check that they really were in the right place.

In our defence, we had warned them all on the invitation what to expect, but I wasn't surprised that they had assumed we were exaggerating.

Beloved Husband gallantly acted as an escort (with a high powered torch) to assist our guests around to the back garden and the patio doors into the house.

The party was a huge success involving several tonnes of pizza, many hours of silly games triggering raucous laughter and some extremely loud music. (My apologies are offered once again to our lovely neighbours! We thank you for your patience.)

Beloved Husband and I eventually escaped to the caravan for a rest, leaving the Barbarians and their friends to their fun. Sometime later on we were called upon to accompany waves of guests back past the crumbly cottage walls to their parents' cars.

All in all a very successful party, but, my goodness we were still tired two days later, so concentrating on what Loss Adjuster Number 2 had to say was not easy.

I rubbed my eyes and tried to focus on what was being discussed.

A fourth (and definitely not the final) issue with regard to repair/rebuild was precisely how much of the cob would need to be removed and rebuilt, and how would the rebuilt section be tied-in to the remaining cob. After all, the cottage originally had four cob walls, only two of which were damaged. There are arguments that cob requires a ring structure in order to remain strong, in other words, all four walls built at the same time in a ring-like formation.

There are no such things as truly straight lines or ninety degree angles in cob, only a vague approximation. Potentially, leaving two walls in-situ and not four constituted a ticking time bomb as they would eventually fail as well.

However as the two remaining walls were not currently crumbling they did not signify as 'needing repair'. Thus the insurance repair job would only extend to the presently damaged walls. If carried out using modern materials these would need to 'tie-in' to the old cob in such a manner that would make all four walls stable. Sticking point number 5. I stopped counting after this, before my brain exploded with too much information. Why was it all so complicated?

An experienced 'old and new building' structural engineer was going to be required. Fortunately we already had one in the form of Genuine Old Buildings Expert. Phew!

Sat at the table in the conservatory listening to Loss Adjuster number 2 explaining, at length, yet more reasons why this situation was so complicated, I have to confess that my mind was really struggling to keep up. I found myself absently watching my boy Barbarians practicing their rugby conversions at the bottom of the garden. In the absence of a set of rugby posts the boys were using the branch of one of the oak trees as a marker for the height of the necessary kick. All progressed as you might expect until I noticed that the smaller Barbarian appeared to be attempting to murder the larger one.

Accidental Damage

Clearing my throat in a meaningful manner I caught Logic's eye in the kitchen and nodded towards the garden. She was just taking a batch of fresh cookies out of the oven. Glancing out in the direction of the boys she grinned in comprehension before leaning over and casually ringing the ship's bell that hangs near the sink. Just once, a short sharp ding!

A significant number of years earlier I had determined that actively calling four Barbarians to the table at meal times before the food went cold was an impossible task, given the size of both the house and the garden.

The A.P.s had solved the problem by donating a ship's bell to the household which meant that in one 'ding' the message that a meal was served could be heard loud and clear by all without me going hoarse in the process. It soon became the most effective method of gaining the whole family's attention for all sorts of reasons if needed, as all would come running immediately. In a family this big you need to be quick if you are going to get your fair share of any snacks.

Therefore, in a response worthy of Pavlov's dog, the instant that the bell rang both boy's heads shot up and the bad behaviour in the garden ceased. Within seconds they were both on their feet and charging for the kitchen slowing up only long enough to slip off muddy shoes and carefully skirt around the meeting taking place at the table. Once in the kitchen Logic allowed the boys to devour still warm cookies whilst muttering quietly to them that they cease and desist in their efforts to commit fratricide while there was an independent witness present in the form of Loss Adjuster Number 2.

I am sure training your children to respond to a bell does not appear in any of the good parenting manuals, but in my defence the adults in the family answer the call too. In fact, at that very meeting when Logic rang the bell for the boys I could see Beloved Husband's involuntary response as his attention was diverted from what Loss Adjuster was saying and he immediately looked towards the kitchen.

Logic took pity on him and brought a plate of fresh cookies over to the table for us too.

Anyway the result of our discussions with Loss Adjuster Number 2 was that another report needed to be done. What a surprise! This one was to establish what potential options were available for a repair at the property. It was to focus on the bare minimum that needed to be put into place to effectively make the property habitable. I do not mean luxuries like carpets, curtains and decorating even though all of that had been damaged by the initial collapse event. The bare minimum meant the repair of the basic structure i.e. the two crumbly walls and nothing else. It was to consider both rebuilding in cob and also modern materials as options.

Once this report was available it was to be sent out to five different building companies for them to come to assess the proposed work identified for the cottage and work out quotes for what the various options would cost. Then the insurance company would decide if they were going to get involved and to what degree.

It was decided that Genuine Old Buildings Expert was suitably qualified to carry out the required report and he was therefore to be commissioned to return to the cottage to assess the potential repair options.

Does your head hurt after reading all that? I am sorry.

I have to admit that I am only explaining these events to the level that I understood them myself. I cannot claim that I had a full grasp of what was actually going on. After this latest meeting I needed to crawl away and have a long lie down to process everything. It didn't really matter though, there would be plenty of time to recover because all those additional reports and assessments were going to take us well into December before any more decisions could be made. What would happen after that was anyone's guess.

I decided that I had better buy more ingredients for my dear Chaos and Logic. We were going to be requiring considerably more edibles.

25: Galvanise

Definition: to stimulate a person into taking action.

Winter looms in the past...

With the approach of December we realised that we were going to be spending Christmas in Hattie. That isn't to say that we didn't receive plenty of offers from other members of the wider family to feed and house us all over the Christmas Holidays. However the Barbarians, Beloved Husband and I came to the conclusion that we wanted to spend the time together just the six of us, and we started to plan exactly what little things we each wanted to do to make our Christmas special, most of which centred inevitably around food.

The onset of winter galvanised me to try to contact Loss Adjuster Number 2 yet again to explain how the weather was penetrating the cottage through the damaged walls and requesting permission to make the useable parts of the house more watertight. The smell of damp from the old section of the house was getting really unpleasant no matter how long we kept the fire lit and I couldn't swear to it but I did wonder if we hadn't gained some little scurrying, fury friends that had made the most of the easy access points available through the walls.

No, I don't mean rats, or I sincerely hoped I didn't!

The spiders had certainly been coming in out of the cold for a while now and I had found several little piles of mouse droppings. I am not really keen on either spiders or mice

Accidental Damage

living with us but at the time there wasn't much that could be done. I couldn't spend my whole life standing on stools and screaming, it didn't really go with the strong independent image I wanted to project to my Barbarians. After all if they spot a weakness then believe me you have had it. (Just to clarify, I am talking about the Barbarians here, not the other wildlife!)

Permission was granted for polythene sheeting to be layered down and around the outside of the damaged walls to prevent much more of the wet weather entering the property.

This was really going to annoy the young postman who delivered our mail to us on a Saturday. I had noticed that he had taken to driving by at speed and just lobbing our parcels through the hole in the wall. If we sealed up the hole he was in danger of having to actually park his van and walk round to the back door to deliver the post like his more mature colleague did during the week. Perhaps I should arrange a basketball net style drop box by the gate for him. It seems a shame to spoil his fun.

At the same time as wrapping the cottage in polythene, the plan included building a small stud wall between the old section of the house and the new, with insulation included so that we would effectively be able to heat the useable parts of the house. The central heating pipework in the damaged walls was to be isolated so that we were not pouring money down the drain trying to heat the great outdoors, whilst simultaneously reducing the chance that exposed pipes would freeze in the coming cold weather and burst.

Following on from this small victory I also mentioned (yet again) that the oil pipe which supplied our central heating boiler was still vulnerable to damage from any falling debris should the crumbly cob collapse any further. I reminded Loss Adjuster Number 2 that I had raised this issue previously because I was afraid that there would be significant environmental damage done if the pipeline broke and oil leaked into the ground. It turned out that this meant yet another assessment would need to be done with regard to what could or should be done.

Oh goody just what we needed, another report!

I wondered if I dare mention the mains electricity supply that was still hanging precariously from the damaged gable. No doubt that needed a report too or it would be feeling ever so left out and we couldn't have that.

With all the reports that were being generated on our behalf I did wonder which forest was being cut down to provide all the paper. I hoped it was a sustainable one. After all there was no guarantee that there would be any actual money to repair the house at the end of all this, any possible budget would potentially have been used up paying all these people to write down their opinions. I suppose we could always screw up all the paper used in these accounts, make spit balls and then cram those into the cracks in the walls. They always proved quite hard for the caretakers to dislodge from the ceilings at school when I was a child (it wasn't me, honest). I am sure the Barbarians would be glad to help out. Anything for a good cause! Might it count as recycling perhaps?

Accidental Damage

In the meantime, while all these lovely commentaries were being written, we simply had to cross our fingers and hope either of the two damaged walls didn't fall any further. Oh! Wait! We were already doing that. Can you cross already crossed fingers?

Is it any wonder that I couldn't sleep? Every day that passed I would pretend to be coping well, brushing off expressions of concern from kind friends with jokey comments, yet at the same time desperately worried that something even worse was around the corner.

I must confess though, that while I was definitely driven by altruistic motives to protect the environment and my beloved Barbarians' lives, I was also rather petrified of the cold showers and chilly rooms that would result if the oil pipeline was damaged and our boiler ceased to function. Self-centred of me I know, but it was really cold enough dashing from Hattie to the house without following it up with an icy cold drenching. Added to that it would only give my boy Barbarians yet another reason to avoid taking a bath and the olfactory essence of their room in Hattie was taking on a personality all of its own already without adding to it unnecessarily.

On the other hand if the pipeline broke and the electricity mains came down at the same time the resultant incendiary combination might be really quite spectacular. That's one way to get warm I suppose! One for the diary anyway or at least You-Tube, so better keep a video camera on standby just in case. I wonder how many hits we would get....

***

While inevitably exhausting, each of these small steps was definitely taking us in the right direction. Even though it felt like every decision had to be written about in triplicate and then discussed by a large committee before anything could actually materialise, at least things were happening. It might seem that very little ground had been covered in more than six months, but every baby step was actually a major victory.

The acknowledgement by the insurance company that we might possibly have a legitimate claim had another fortuitous knock on effect. Even though there was no guaranteed repair offer on the table, the fact that they were in communication with us, meant that Beloved Husband was able to justifiably approach the mortgage company with regard to releasing some additional funds for us to put towards 'home improvements' that might take place whilst any repair work was going on.

Thus a modest sum was agreed which we would be able to use to contribute towards whatever work might be needed. As a result both Beloved Husband and I felt as though we had a little bit more control over the painfully slow proceedings. We didn't of course, (it's not as if it was our house or anything like that, heaven forbid that ownership should come into this!) but it was nice to pretend we did.

I would be dishonest if I didn't confess at this point that it seemed to me that everyone else involved in our situation was making quite a tidy living out it. It is probably not remotely true but from our perspective it appeared to be a nice little earner for all concerned apart from us, so you can understand my frustration as yet more delays for assessments and reports appeared at every turn.

Accidental Damage

I just wanted to scream "For goodness' sake! It fell down!! It needs fixing!!! Please can we just get ON WITH IT???!!!!"

26: <u>Oblivion</u>
Definition: A state of total unawareness

Back in my more luxurious future, I was floating in a blissful cloud of colour, beautiful rainbow shades swirling in a cascading waterfall as I became aware of another sensation. Instead of visual this one was auditory, but was just as lovely.

The sound of gentle piano playing penetrated my painting fog. It was a sound I recognised. It was truly lovely and made me smile. Drifting back to full consciousness I was aware that something about the music didn't make sense.

Both of my beautiful Barbarian girls play the piano, but they each have their own very distinctive style and musical preference. This particular piece did not fit with the acknowledged female Barbarian that was currently in residence at home, and thus required investigating. After all the boys don't play the piano, what a ridiculous suggestion! It requires far too much concentration and focus when there are snacks to be unearthed, brothers to wrestle to the ground for no reason and random balls to be chased!

Hurriedly washing off my paintbrush in the jar of murky water on the desk, I dumped it on the scrap of towel beside the jar and went to delve into the apparent mystery. For once the radio wasn't playing and the cat had abandoned her sunny windowsill. There was definitely something afoot!

Stepping into the hall I could see that I was right, tinkling away on the ivories of the old upright by the stairs was the Princess of Chaos herself, playing her signature tune. She had written it herself during the caravan years. It sounds like a joyfully, flowing stream, skipping down a mountainside and it brings tears of happiness to my eyes every time I hear it. Possibly my all-time favourite piece and the reason I had known for certain that Logic was not playing. (Not that I'm saying she doesn't play beautifully too, of course!)

Torn between delight at seeing her yet also wondering what on earth she was doing here and confused as to how she had managed to get home from university without parental assistance, I watched her finish the piece with a flourish. She turned to me, bounced off the piano stool and gave me a quick hug.

"Hey Ma, you look happy!" she said. "Don't worry lectures are cancelled today and tomorrow too. It's because the January exams are over. It gives the lecturers time to mark everything. We start back Monday, so that gives me four days at home."

I nodded absorbing the rapid fire information stream and hugged her back. I couldn't help smiling.

"One of the guys in my hall was driving home for the weekend so I persuaded him to make a slight detour to drop me off. He's coming back Sunday to pick me up, I said you'd feed him Sunday Lunch in place of petrol money, you don't mind do you?"

Turning to go into the kitchen to put on the kettle I hid a huge grin. Chaos' powers of persuasion are legendary in this family so the poor fella from her halls hadn't stood a chance. I imagine that her 'slight detour' was probably quite considerable as we do live on the backside of beyond.

There's no doubt he would truly deserve a nice dinner when he got here on Sunday, if, indeed, he ever found us again. Besides, when you are cooking for a horde this big, one more mouth to feed is never a problem.

"Anyway," she continued without an answer, she is also notorious for not necessarily needing any verbal feedback to carry on a conversation, "I thought I would take the opportunity to check out your new paintings."

"And possibly get your washing done?" I asked innocently having just spotted the huge rucksack quietly steaming away by the utility door.

"Yeah, the laundrette at my hall is out of order. Sorry! You don't mind do you?"

"Be my guest," I said setting down two cups of tea on the counter top. "Just remember the forty five minute, thirty degrees setting is the only one that actually still works."

Sipping my tea I watched through the open utility door as she up-ended her rucksack spilling the rather rancid contents onto the stone floor and started shoving armfuls into my poor, beleaguered washing machine. It really should have been given a long service medal and copious amounts of danger money coming to work in this house. It had slowly given up all hope of operating any of its fancy, sophisticated, higher wash functions, settling for the basic fast-wash facility on an extremely regular basis. There was never any time for anything else. Even that one working setting was a bit hit-and-miss, but there was no money for a new machine and anyway I felt rather attached to this one. It had come through the caravan years with us, and I felt we could put up with its little foibles.

Nevertheless, looking at the festering contents of Chaos' rucksack I wondered if this might just be the final straw for my poor machine and couldn't help but speculate on how on earth I would cope if it decided to go on strike permanently.

My conjecture was interrupted by the shrill tones of the landline. Picking it up, I listened carefully to the caller, before agreeing several times, saying goodbye and then disconnecting the call.

Inveterately nosey, Chaos was out of the utility like a shot, wanting to know what was going on.

"What was that?" she asked as I sat staring at the handset with a bemused expression on my face.

I looked at her for several seconds before I found my voice. "Apparently, I've sold a painting!"

"Really? That's great! Which one? I didn't think there were any left from the old lot."

"I am not really sure," I said. "I lent several to a friend a few years ago. She was setting up her own business and wanted some art on the office walls. She didn't have a huge budget and I had a few pieces available. There was no point them staying in the shed when someone was offering them wall space so I let her borrow them if she would agree to put a price tag on them. I had forgotten all about them to be honest."

"Wow, that's great, how much?" asked the eternally poverty-stricken student.

"Enough to replace that washing machine, if you kill it with your rucksack of rankness!" I said with some degree of satisfaction.

It might be the end of the line for the whining, wheezing washer, but not for the rest of us just yet.

As we were all probably going to live, a little bit longer at least, I thought I had better turn my mind to planning, and shopping, for a suitably stimulating Sunday lunch to restore Chaos' friend if he did eventually successfully locate us. Once again my cupboards were looking worryingly sparse. How does that happen?

Please understand that I would never claim to be a Michelin Starred Chef. (Beloved Husband would die laughing if I tried and we wouldn't want that! Would we? Hmmm...) Nevertheless, the one thing I can do really well is a Sunday Roast.

In truth I must credit Delia with the overall continued survival of my brood of Barbarians. My entrenched position as chief cook and bottle washer for this tribe has not been easily earned. They would not have endured half as well as they have, were it not for Delia Smith's Complete Illustrated Cookery Course which resides on my kitchen shelf in dilapidated splendour, wearing just a splash (if not considerably more) of virtually every dish I have ever attempted to make.

Accidental Damage

My heartfelt thanks must go to my cousin and his lovely wife who gifted the book to us as a wedding present. Beloved Husband was in no danger of dying of starvation when we first got married because of the plentiful variety of excellent takeaway establishments within easy reach of our first home. The original home with good solid foundations and nice, strong, concrete walls! Why on earth did we sell it?

However once the Barbarians started arriving and we moved to the deepest darkest depths of the countryside he had to survive on my culinary skills alone even though they could more accurately be referred to as my incineration skills?

It's just as well for all of us that in the intervening years I have learned to cook. This happened in the same rapidly exponential manner that the Barbarians learned to eat and I now have no qualms about throwing together vast banquets of edible shenanigans. Nothing fancy mind you, just good, honest, wholesome, nourishing food.

With regard to that good, honest, wholesome, nourishing food, it was time yet again to raid an ingredients establishment.

27: <u>Resilience</u>

Definition: the ability to survive in spite of change or misfortune

Meanwhile back in the past at the house of fun we were being visited by yet more experts. This time our visitors were construction experts (a.k.a. builders) a whole series of them, arriving one after another, all ostensibly coming to quote for the potential work ahead. Although, some I felt were really just there to be nosey as our house was now notorious far and wide. (I told you we should have been selling tickets.)

Who cares? At last, after nearly six months we had builders at the property. Yay, result!!!

Builders, hooray, I hear you shout!

Do calm down! It was not really a cause for mass celebration. They weren't staying long enough to actually rebuild the place. They were simply assessing the potential cost of a series of rebuild scenarios determined by one of the many previously generated engineering reports from Genuine Old Buildings Expert.

Nevertheless it was yet another baby step forward. (When is this baby going to learn to run? Can't we skip walking, we really don't have time?)

Of course, as with everything else in this whole messy scenario, it wasn't actually easy to show builders inside a tumble down property. This was especially so, now that the huge crack in the wall had been sealed over with thick black polythene. Believe me, there was no way I was going to let anyone cut a route in through that if I could help it. It was the middle of winter and the polythene was one of the few things keeping the true extent of the miserable, wet, cold weather from joining us on the inside of the house.

The original front door of the cottage was now wedged shut, not intentionally so, but rather more due to the sheer weight of the damaged wall suspended over it pressing down under the influence of gravity. Added to that complication, the only internal access from the back section of the house had been boarded up with more plastic sheeting, plywood and thick insulation materials. Again, I wasn't having that dismantled in a hurry either. Thus entry for inspection was not going to be a walk in the park.

Fortunately we had anticipated that access might be an issue and had left a downstairs window in the undamaged side wall unlocked for this very purpose. Unusually for a cottage, it was a rather large window and lifted upwards from about mid-thigh height, allowing our callers to scramble over the sill and access the ground floor. I have to admit I had never in my life thought we would be encouraging guests to clamber into our home through a window, but it just goes to show that anything is possible given the right set of circumstances.

Understandably, with the majority of the front section of the house encased in black plastic and the fried electrical circuits turned off, it was rather dark inside the old cottage, necessitating the deployment of independent light sources. Thus each group tended to look rather like a bunch of miners about to descend to the bowels of the earth with head torches attached to hard hats, the only missing equipment was the traditional pickaxe.

Once inside the cottage it was quite evident to both Beloved Husband and me, even by torch light, that very gradual, incremental movement was still merrily underway. The previously charmingly characteristic low ceiling was now distinctly more low-slung, meaning that everyone (even me, at the lofty height of five foot two inches) had to bend over to walk towards the stair well at the far end of the room, to prevent banging heads on the straining beams. Large chunks of internal plasterwork littered the floor, and the smell of damp and mould was over powering. Derelict and depressed our dear old cottage was dying before our eyes.

Needless to say these internal examinations got briefer and briefer with each subsequent arrival mainly due to the sheer impracticalities involved. Nevertheless each new builder, arriving to assess the situation, insisted on attempting to take internal photographs even though we warned them that the last lot of builders' photographic attempts were useless due to the poor lighting conditions.

Beloved Husband and I eventually become rather used to not existing to these people. It was as if we were an encumbrance to be endured, a nuisance, and so we gave up accompanying them inside the derelict ruin of our home, and resorted to just counting them in through the window and then out again afterwards.

The contractors wanted the work but seemed to know that we were irrelevant in the decision making process and hence they were focussed entirely on communicating with Genuine Old Buildings Expert and, through him, the insurance company.

Accidental Damage

Even Genuine Old Buildings Expert, who was in theory supposed to have been engaged as a neutral third party to communicate between the insurance company and us with regard to the project, was still actually paid by the insurance company. As a result, while he was an extremely nice chap with the very best of intentions, he seemed unable to involve us particularly in any decisions. Communication was kept to the bare minimum. We were simply informed what was going to happen once decisions had already taken place.

This was actually quite unfortunate, if you ask me (and nobody was asking me – we've established that) because the insurance company were still adamant that they were only potentially considering accepting liability for the bare minimum repair on the cottage. Yet it should be remembered that critical decisions made at this point were going to affect the amount of actual work that needed to take place and would significantly affect the final repair bill which ultimately would be down to us to pay.

All the delays in decision making were allowing the cottage to fall in to even greater disrepair leading to an exponentially increasing ultimate invoice which again would inevitably be presented to us for payment.

In short we couldn't help but feel marginalised by the system, which fitted very well with the other helpless, hopeless and totally powerless feelings overwhelming us. We were like a cork bobbing in the ocean being blown this way and that by the winds over the surface of the water whilst simultaneously tugged at from below by the currents, defenceless and vulnerable.

"Do you think they actually see us?" I muttered to Beloved Husband one day after holding the window up for yet another set of contractors to scramble through.

He just shrugged and raised his eyebrows. I closed the window and sat on the low wall nearby waiting for this latest bunch of builders to knock and ask to be let out again. He sat next to me and we rested shoulder to shoulder in companionable silence watching our breath generate frost clouds in the air until eventually he gently shoved my shoulder with his and said in a remarkably cheerful tone, "I guess lots of builders is better than none."

"Hmmm," I agreed, thinking distractedly that his comment was an indication that Beloved Husband was perhaps trying to see things in a glass-half-full capacity just as I was tipping into glass-half-empty territory. Looking back on that horrible time it is interesting to observe how the dynamics between the two of us fluctuated. How, on the whole, one of us would carry the other at different times. Although both of us had been brought very low by the whole ordeal, whichever of us was feeling slightly brighter would instinctively try to bolster up the other.

Fortunately there were very few moments when we were both reaching complete and utter despair together and at those points our lovely Barbarians were instrumental in keeping us both going. Whether their more comical antics were deliberately designed to revitalise us, I will never know, but somehow our little team managed to sustain itself, each protecting and encouraging the other.

Quite shockingly one of the very last builders to visit the site at that time actually spoke to us! He asked us what we thought should be done. We were pathetically grateful to be consulted about the future of our own property and he seemed genuinely interested in our opinions. Quite a contrast to those who had come before! Such a shame we probably weren't going to get a choice as to which builder would get the job in the end, because with that one simple conversation he just beat all the others hands down as far as we were concerned.

Eventually the steady stream of visiting builders dried up and we were left in peace to wait for a few more weeks while they went away and compiled their reports for submission as tenders for the potential repair work.

***

When I say we were left in peace, I am lying of course.

What I mean is that we were abandoned yet again to worry about how things were going to unfold. Sleepless nights were standard. Hours spent lying awake in the dark pretending to sleep so that I wouldn't disturb anyone else, with collapsing-building-related disaster movies playing on a loop in my head to visibly demonstrate to me just how much worse our present situation could potentially get. (I have already admitted to a hefty dose of paranoia!)

I rather think that my obsession was rather justifiable considering preceding events. After all there are certain disasters in life that one can mitigate for. For example, if one fears a home fire then it is reasonable to take the time to turn off electrical items after use, especially before leaving the house for any length of time.

Obviously turning electrical products off doesn't give 100% protection from a home fire but it certainly improves your odds of such an event not happening.

So it would stand to reason when buying a house that if you have had a full structural survey which indicates that all is in good order, and you carry out all appropriate standard building maintenance and repairs in good time and to a high standard, you don't usually spend time worrying about your house collapsing. This is a fundamentally rock solid basis for your personal sense of home security.

Until one day it does actually fall down.

Then believe me, any potential disaster is up for grabs.

Therefore I don't think I was really that mad to be a touch obsessed about the oil pipe. Especially as every single one of the builders who had visited the site to inspect the damaged walls had said to me cheerfully and, I felt, rather patronisingly, "You want to watch that oil pipe, love," as they trotted past it.

(I was trying to get it watched but no one was listening!)

It eventually struck me during one of those painfully long, dark, sleepless nights that we were approaching the situation from the wrong angle. The oil pipe was admittedly in danger. There was no doubt about that. I had warned the insurance company about it yet they were fairly non-committal and I now realised why.

They didn't see that it was their problem.

Accidental Damage

You see! I said I wasn't that bright, it takes me a while but I do get there in the end.

Now, I have already admitted to significant sleep deprivation by this point, so I do not actually know if the following is factually correct. Nevertheless it occurred to me that the pipe hadn't actually been damaged yet, and as I had foreseen that it might get damaged and informed them of this, then, they could very easily turn round to me in the event that it was ultimately severed by further slippage and ask me why I hadn't taken action to sort it out.

Catch 22 perhaps?

I would argue that the damage was caused by the falling wall. They would no doubt respond that I could have, (in fact I already had) predicted the damage and therefore should have done something to prevent it. I could argue that they should have listened to me and advised me what action to take, but they could counter that it wasn't their problem until it actually happens, and even though I do have oil spill cover in my policy, because I didn't have accidental damage or some other such cover I was probably not protected.

In short, I didn't really expect them to help.

Paranoid? Me? Not at all, I am now a realist.

Or is that a fatalist?

Hmmm...! Anyway, do you blame me? Still, let's not get side tracked. While I don't actually know if this is what would really happen, it was entirely possible that we could ultimately argue until we were blue in the face with oil pouring into the ground and the Environment Agency issuing a big fat fine.

I was still pretty certain that that bill would land on our door mat too. After all they do say misery loves company and we were pretty miserable.

I wasn't prepared to go there as I simply didn't have the energy.

Oil is always a fairly slippery subject, but in all of the years that we lived in the country we found that it was the simplest, most economical and efficient way to heat our home, regardless of which fuel crisis the government was bleating on about at the time.

I have to confess when we first moved to this remote location I was concerned about not being on mains gas. I wondered just how we were going to maintain a constant supply of fuel. Surely, we would run out just when we needed it the most? After all, knowing our luck, (as by now you should) it would have to be the coldest day in the darkest winter, just as all our pipes are in danger of freezing instantly if you don't have your heating on, that our oil supply would give up the ghost.

Yes, I know, my pessimistic streak is showing again. Sorry! I will try and put it away.

As it happens most tanks can be fitted with this very clever device which comes free from the oil supplier, giving them an electronic reading on the level of oil in your tank at all times so that as soon as the fuel level drops below a certain amount they send a nice chap with a tanker load and fill it up for you. You pay a monthly amount, just as you would to a gas company, and everyone is happy, and more importantly warm!

The location of your oil tank is generally very carefully considered. After all there are all sorts of rules to govern where they can go even though many properties struggle to conform to all of them, mainly because they are quite contradictory, as all truly efficient guidelines should be.

It's no fun otherwise.

As a result our tank site is to the far side of our property, away from the cottage, the thatch, the garage and all of the sheds. It is not too close to the flammable wooden fencing and there are no overhanging trees or wood stores nearby. An excellent location you might think, apart from the fact that it is quite a long way away from our actual boiler, the bathrooms and the mains water supply.

Not a problem! That's why we have an oil pipeline. If laid with sufficient fall then gravity can enable an uninterrupted supply of oil to flow from your tank along a substantial length of pipe to your boiler. Usually this pipe would be laid close to major structures such as the base of a house or even partly buried underground to give it some protection from inadvertent damage. So it came to be that our pipeline ran along the base of the cottage wall, around the corner to the boiler. Thus in our precarious house-falling-down situation the oil pipe was in prime location for maximum potential damage should either or both walls succumb to gravity.

The last thing we needed (apart from obviously not wanting to be the source of any environmental damage) right then were yet more financial threats in the form of potential fines looming over us. So I am sure you can understand just how concerned we were about the situation. It felt like a sword of Damocles was hanging over us, or at least hanging over our oil pipe, and we needed to get it sorted.

The final straw, as it always seems to, came after yet another windy night. You would be forgiven for thinking that we lived in a hurricane alley or something, the number of storms I keep wittering on about. I can assure you we don't it is just that those couple of winters were very volatile.

That particular night some of the black sheeting that had encased the damaged cottage came lose at one end and flapped like an untethered sail all night while the caravan rocked alarmingly. We spent the night wondering what would happen first, either the house would take off or Hattie would, to be found half a mile away in the morning messing up someone's duck pond.

Yet, as before, a sleepless and stormy night resulted in a morning of action. Beloved Husband and I decided to take matters into our own hands. The laptop was redeployed and a further email sent to the insurance company telling them that in the absence of any response from them, we were going to make our own arrangements to prevent an oil spill on the property. This was followed by a bit of research and the purchase of a new oil tank.

You might wonder why a new tank was necessary. Surely we were over reacting, could we not move the one we had?

Accidental Damage

Now that would be far too easy.

Haven't you been listening?

We don't do easy here.

The answer to your question is no, for several reasons. The principle one being that the rules wouldn't allow us to. Our tank was not of the most recent design. While made of the appropriately thick plastic material required and in excellent condition, it was not what is referred to as 'bunded'. This means that it should effectively be two tanks, one inside the other so that if the inner wall fails for whatever reason there is a second wall to prevent oil egress. How you tell if your inner wall has failed I don't know but I assume there is a clever bit of electronic kit that will inform you.

So our tank didn't comply with the latest regulations. While it remained in situ it was perfectly OK to continue using it. However if it was to be moved then we were obliged by those pesky government imperatives to install the latest acceptable design. Hence a new tank was unavoidable as we were planning to move both tank and pipeline temporarily round to the other side of the property so that they were no longer at risk.

Your next question, if you are paying attention and haven't got bored and wandered off to make a cup of tea, (I wouldn't blame you if you have, I'd have loved to be able to escape all of this.) might be why move the tank at all, why not simply re-route the pipeline away from the damaged walls?

Excellent suggestion! Well done, you are still awake after all that aren't you? I am impressed.

Unfortunately we had already considered this and had a quote as to whether this might be possible. It wasn't. The distance around the back of the house was simply too far and did not permit sufficient fall or drop to allow the oil to flow efficiently as far as the boiler. Shame really, as this would have been a nice cheap and easy, temporary solution.

From a practical point of view the presence of a second tank made the move far easier as it meant that the new tank could be installed before the old tank was decommissioned, allowing all the oil to then be decanted across from one to the other, and there was a lot of oil to move.

Having made the decision to act we were able to order a new tank within minutes, thanks to the internet. It would be delivered in four days' time and could be plumbed in two days after that, which would leave us the weekend to spend decanting oil from one tank to the other. We had elected to do this fun job ourselves as it would keep the bill to a minimum and the pennies were definitely not in a plentiful supply.

Thus exactly eight days later and our potential oil spill disaster had been averted. The new tank was installed and fully operational. The old tank was retained in the hope that it could be used for the whole process to be repeated in reverse should we ever successfully repair the house and be able to move the new tank back around to the original tank's location, after which we planned for the old one to be appropriately recycled as per the local authority's regulations. Beloved Husband and I made use of our still functioning boiler to generate copious quantities of hot water for a lengthy shower or ten, because, take my word for it, oil does not wash off easily. There is a certain odious quality that lingers long after contact and generates some very odd looks in the queue for the village post office on a Monday morning, or so I found.

PART 6

A wise individual does not allow their future to be stolen by the events of the past.

28: <u>Teamwork</u>

Definition: the collective action of a group of people operating collaboratively towards a mutual goal.

Once again, back in the present, dabbing away at a wet canvas in my little hidey hole I became aware of a peaceful quiet within the house around me.

This sounded a dim warning bell.

Early life with the Barbarians had led me to be highly suspicious of silence. It usually meant that mischief was underway. Even now that they were growing up into surprisingly civilised individuals I couldn't suppress an instinctive distrust of tranquillity. In addition to the stillness I noted the conspicuous absence of my usual sugary sustenance, which was rather peculiar too and definitely required investigation.

So just to be on the safe-side I sidled over to the door, brush in hand, and peered along the corridor towards the kitchen.

Aha! Interesting!

Logic had obviously welcomed the temporary return of Chaos to the family home and they were both contentedly coating my kitchen surfaces with a variety of sticky, sugar-related substances as they slipped back into their customary roles of culinary creation. That would explain the absence of my mid-morning snack. It was probably still in the oven.

The peace and quiet was due to the fact that each Barbarian was plugged into a separate I-pod and silently nodding along to their individual choice of auditory entertainment, obviously content to be together but not necessarily requiring any form of verbal exchange. They always did seem to read each other's minds, which is quite an achievement for two such unique personalities.

Smiling I retreated back to my canvas where a bright array of summer flowers were blooming.

If the girls were content, I could safely assume the boys were suitably occupied. I knew from past experience that Chaos and Logic would be very quick to stomp loudly on any outrageous Barbarian boy behaviour, and the boys wouldn't dream of stepping out of line if there were freshly baked cookies in the offing.

Rather than interfere I returned to enthusiastically splodging a selection of scarlet snap dragons across my colourful canvas all the while contemplating how lovely it was to see my beautiful daughters enjoying each other's company once again. They had missed each other.

Our little family unit was changing, with one Barbarian having left home already and the second soon to follow. This was a gradual modification. Our team was adapting to the change naturally and not being brutally and prematurely ripped apart like it had so nearly been two years previously. This change was a healthy one and we were handling it well so far.

Thinking back over our time in the caravan I marvelled at what situations you can adapt to if you are willing to put your mind to it. Once what had previously passed for 'normal life' had been thrown out of the window, our

Accidental Damage

Barbarians were very quick to start pulling together as a team.

In the early days of our little family's creation, as with all sibling groups there were inevitable tussles and power struggles. Brothers and sisters never fully appreciate each other's finer points until they start to grow up a bit. However living through the disastrous loss of our home and the potential destruction of our family life, as well as surviving the close confines of caravan life for an extended period of time, seemed to have brought a significant maturity to their overall approach to life that any parent would be proud of.

It had been fascinating to watch them thinking up ways to make our new garden-based existence generally easier for all. For example astonishing levels of collaboration went into things like establishing a boosted internet connection that would reach Hattie from the house enabling them to each engage in electronic endeavours without having to trot back to the house to gain a connection.

They also seemed to pay far more attention to what was going on around them, although this was in all probability due to the fact that when you are living with five other people in a 35 foot by 12 foot metal box you can't really ignore anything, or anyone, effectively.

Nevertheless they obviously noticed which general day to day jobs were so much harder to achieve during that instalment of our life and I was always grateful to accept any offers of help that came my way. They were all suddenly quite content to carry things to and from Hattie and the house for me, when it would never previously have occurred to the Barbarians to offer to carry anything anywhere, be it taking clean washing upstairs or lifting the vacuum cleaner downstairs, without me first employing a verbal three line whip. (OK, I really mean 'indulging in a hissy fit'!)

On occasion Beloved Husband I had even observed them co-operating to help each other carry necessary paraphernalia back and forth.

So, all in all, life in Hattie did have its good points. Not that I am recommending it to anyone you understand.

****

Anyway, returning to the student and the wet washing in the future....

Later that day, following the consumption of the most delicious still-warm chocolate brownies, I was helping Chaos to distribute her wet undergarments along the radiators in the conservatory listening to her chattering away about university life. As usual she didn't really require a verbal response from me and I was just enjoying having her at home for a fleeting visit regardless of the significant increase in damp laundry that now festooned the house.

She was telling me about how she and some friends had recently signed a contract to rent a house for their second year and was describing the property to me in detail. One comment in particular caught my attention.

Whilst telling me that the house was a fairly new property, with double glazing, five double bed rooms, no obvious damp, etcetera, she said earnestly, "It does seem stable enough!"

Accidental Damage

I had a flash of pity for the rental estate agent. I bet they had never come across a student like Chaos before. Most young people probably stressed about who was going to get the biggest bedroom or how many bathrooms were available or if bills were included in the rental price. Whereas Chaos had probably demanded to see a recent full structural survey and asked if there was any evidence of subsidence in the area. I wouldn't have put it past her to check if the garden was large enough to accommodate a static caravan too, just in case.

Our home collapse had no doubt had a lasting effect, both positive and negative, on all of our beloved Barbarians.

Yet hopefully, at the same time perhaps they had gained true knowledge about their strength of self, and the value of teamwork to overcome significant odds along with basics things like learning to always check the small print on your insurance documents.

29: <u>Conclusion</u>
Definition: A decision based on reasoning.

Back to the messy situation in the past...

We eventually settled into an unusual but comforting domestic routine. We were getting rather used to our unconventional existence with its cosy and companionable evenings around the fire in the house before making a chilly bedtime dash to the caravan armed with hot water bottles, fleecy dressing gowns and waterproofs just in case. Interestingly, for the first time in their lives the Barbarians were discovering the point of the slippers I have always buought them, especially now that the patio flagstones more often than not sported a thin layer of ice, courtesy of Jack Frost, in both the evenings and the early mornings.

Although we were very grateful for the protection that Hattie's arrival had afforded the family unit, prolonged periods of time spent in the caravan rooms felt immensely claustrophobic, especially now that winter was on us and all doors and windows had to remain closed to retain any available heat. Thus it had become habit to stay together in the house by the fire until the last possible moment to go to bed and hopefully straight to sleep.

The result was actually very pleasant as we would sit together sometimes watching TV as a group or at other times each engaged in our own individual tasks thanks to judicious use of headphones, laptops and I-pads etc. As a result A-level studies and last minute homework could take place alongside cartoons, rom-coms or televised sporting events. It proved to be a very companionable and cosy way for a large group of mixed ages to spend the evenings.

The boys soon learned to take advantage of the almost permanently lit open fire to work out what snacks could be warmed, toasted or occasionally incinerated over it.

Having unearthed an old fashioned toasting fork during the main house clearance they started out with simple things like scorching marshmallows and progressed through cremating slices of bread to transforming chipolata sausages into charcoal sticks. Then the real fun began as they moved on to making actual filled toasties in a home-made contraption they had devised themselves out of two broken, metal sieves stolen from my kitchen. (I have my suspicions that my sieves weren't actually broken prior to the Barbarians getting their hands on them but learned a long time ago not to ask questions that I probably didn't want the answers to. This was one of those occasions.)

Having assembled the complicated contents of their sandwiches they would clamp them between the flattened metal netting sections of the sieves and using an extended handle they would hold the whole contrivance over the fire for the bread to brown on first one side and then the other.

It took several goes to get it right at first but eventually their offerings were really very edible indeed. The contents of the toasties would melt into a pleasing and warming evening delicacy that the rest of the family were queuing up to consume. Even some of the more outlandish combinations of flavours that Quiet created were willingly ingested.

This certainly kept the boys well occupied throughout the chilly winter evenings and meant that any form of formal supper was not really necessary as someone had to eat the results of each experimental phase. There was even a scoring system based firstly on how successfully the snack stayed together during the toasting phase and then on the overall taste. Points were lost for partial disintegration or complete loss of snack to the flames below.

Who needs reality TV? We had 'come toast with me', an altogether far more brilliant and explorative form of untried TV viewing. (£200,000 remember?) It was amazing just how inventive the evening culinary exploits became. Move over Jamie Oliver, the Barbarian Boys have arrived!

It was during such an evening as this, a few days before Christmas, that I noticed Beloved Husband suddenly freeze with a fairly mundane cheese, ham, pepperoni, mayonnaise and pickle toasty half way to his mouth. His eyes were staring fixedly at his laptop screen. Concerned that he might either be choking or actually having a seizure I abandoned my own plate, hurriedly extracted myself from the pile of floor cushions near the fire (the best location in my opinion to simultaneously stay warm and get first refusal on the most successful looking snacks) and crossed over to the sofa to see what the problem might be.

Having ascertained that he was indeed breathing just fine and also fully conscious I realised that something in his e-mail had caught his attention. Nosy as always, I read it over his shoulder and gave a squeak. He turned his head and we looked at each other with eyebrows raised in surprise.

Accidental Damage

Obviously, in a family like ours, this odd behaviour wasn't going to go unnoticed for long.

"Well?" demanded Logic having extracted her headphones from both ears.

Beloved Husband looked questioningly at me and I shrugged.

"It's an email from the house insurance company," he said.

"OK, what reports do they want to do now? Surely there's nothing left they can possibly assess, or do they want second opinions on everything next?" Chaos said dryly.

"No, far from it, it would seem that they have finally made a decision," he said.

"And?" said Quiet.

"It doesn't say. Apparently we have to wait. The Professional Gentleman is going to telephone us to let us know."

"So their second refusal won't be in writing I suppose," Chaos huffed. "That won't stop us going to the financial ombudsman though."

"Does it give you any idea when he might phone you?" Logic asked. "Is it likely to be before Christmas?"

"I shouldn't think so!" I said.

Alice May

There was silence, apart from some significant hissing and spitting from a forgotten cheese sandwich in the fire, as we all looked at each other apprehensively.

Suddenly the telephone rang.

All six of us jumped and then leapt for the handset at once with Beloved Husband winning by a country mile. (Longer legs you see. He is such a cheat!)

From the tangled heap on the floor where the rest of us had landed after he shoved us all aside in his haste to get to the handset first, we listened transfixed to his side of the conversation, which was extremely uninformative and went something like this.

"Hello."

Pause.

"Yes."

Pause.

"Yes."

Pause.

"O.K."

Pause.

"Uh huh."

Accidental Damage

Pause.

"OK."

I'll stop there. It went on like that for quite a while but I am sure you get the general picture.

Not very illuminating.

Rather a shame he was not using the speaker phone but I suppose he was trying to spare the Barbarians from what was probably bad news. Although from the hissed exchange passing between the two girls, they had already assumed it was bad anyway, (as had I).

After a few more "yes"s and another couple of "OK"s there was a "bye" and Beloved Husband lowered the phone and stood stock still in absolute silence.

Ah!

He was looking rather shocked.

He didn't make any attempt to speak although his mouth did open and close a few times. Unfortunately he seemed unable to summon any sound at all. (Please don't tell me that we were returning to the days of living with a verbally challenged ostrich, I really don't think I could cope with that again.)

"It's OK!" I said encouragingly, jumping to my feet and stepping over a few Barbarians to reach him. "Don't worry! We knew they would probably refuse to help us."

"No!" he managed to mutter shaking his head in disbelief. Surely he couldn't really have thought that there was much chance that they were going to help us.

"Don't worry, Dad," chimed in Logic scrambling out from under Small.

"Get them to put their refusal in writing and we can appeal," I said standing right in front of him. "It's wicked to do it over the phone so we can't appeal."

"No!" he said urgently, looking at me with a wild expression in his eyes.

'Oh heck,' I thought, 'he's really lost it this time.' With Beloved Husband struggling to form more than that one word (obviously complete sentences were out of the question) it must be incredibly bad news.

"It's alright, Dad!" Chaos added. "The letter to the Financial Ombudsman is already written. We finished it last week."

"Yes," I said, "It's just waiting for the details of the second refusal and then we can send it straight away."

"No!" he said grabbing hold of my shoulders, "Stop!" (That was another word. Progress! Excellent!)

"Stop what?" I asked confused.

"Stop talking!" he said giving me a gentle shake. "Let me think!"

"OK" I said, "but can you hurry up please?"

Accidental Damage

After a few seconds he took a deep breath and said "It's going to be OK!"

"I know! That's what I said! If you can...." I tailed off when he gave me a look. (Ooops, I was still talking.)

I shrugged mutely back at him apologetically.

We all stood looking at him in total silence for a few seconds before he took a deep breath and smiled (the first real smile I had seen from him in more than six months) and he said "It's going to be OK, because the insurance company have agreed to the basic repair! Apparently the builders start in January!"

30: <u>Hero</u>

Definition: A person who, in the opinion of others, has heroic qualities

Two years after that momentous telephone call, I was surprised to find myself humming along to the radio while doing a happy little jig. While I am not allowed to name the song due to copyright laws, if you think of the happiest song to grace our airwaves in recent years then you can probably guess what I am listening to.

My goodness! What a change! Here I was practically dancing.

Looking about me I had to admit that I really couldn't refer to this particular room as anything other than a studio now, no matter how hard I tried. It was not a study or a cubby hole or a spare room anymore. The filing cabinet, a shelving unit and two chairs had been evicted and the space was now stacked full of finished canvases. I had to accept that my painting was back to stay, so an 'art studio' it was!

I was contemplating the vast amount of artwork that I had generated in the last few weeks. There was more than enough here for an exhibition if I ever felt like putting physical evidence of my desperate climb back up from the depths of complete emotional disintegration on public display. Perhaps not eh! Demonic daffodils and such are not everyone's cup of tea. However, I felt my silver fish, swimming determinedly upwards from the deep oceanic abyss were quite optimistic, even rather inspiring. This particular image marked a very positive turning point in my recovery and I had painted several different variations on that theme in the end, as they were so enjoyably relaxing to create.

The musical paintings definitely had potential, too, especially if they were framed up as a pretty and colourful orchestral series. The bright, vibrancy practically danced off the canvases with joy even though I do say so myself.

A small sound and the appearance of a steaming cup and a plate of cake by my elbow made me turn. Expecting my intruder to be Logic, I was pleasantly surprised to see Beloved Husband standing next to me. Ah! It had never occurred to me that he might be the source of any of the sustaining snacks that kept mysteriously appearing recently? Was he the one who had been looking after me all this time that I had been mentally wandering through the past?

My own personal superhero brandishing fresh cake and a hot cuppa, what more could a girl want? (White knights on powerful steads are all very well but I've always thought that the armour and horse hair, not to mention the egos would get in the way?)

I met his eyes enquiringly. "You've been busy!" he commented casually.

"Hmmm!" I agreed.....

"Are you feeling any better yet?" he asked.

I regarded him steadily but didn't reply.

"You seem better," he continued carefully, "happier? Have you managed to work some things out?"

I nodded, looking down at the paintings spread all around me and smiled.

"Dare we hope that you have finally forgiven yourself then?" he said.

Startled, I looked up at him but quickly looked away again in confusion. I don't know why I was so surprised really. He has always had this peculiar ability to know what is on my mind. (No, he is not literally reading my mind word for word, but he pays far more attention than you would think, and he's probably the only person on the planet who actually remotely understands me. Poor chap!) I have been quite grumpy, so it probably wasn't that difficult to put two and two together.

"You do know that none of us have ever blamed you for what happened, don't you?" he persevered. "We've all said so. Many times, but you won't listen. You just keep on holding yourself accountable, way more than anyone else would or even could."

There was a moment of silence as I gathered my wits, before I gave a deep sigh and spoke. "If I had not made that mistake with the insurance right at the start, things would have been so different."

"Not necessarily," he said. "You don't know that, none of us do. I have a feeling that everyone has a bit of a battle on their hands with any big insurance claim. It's inevitable that you have to justify any sizeable application for funds, and this was a pretty big claim. It's different if it's just a broken TV or a window pane. Anyway it wasn't accidental damage in the end was it? That definition was irrelevant. Whether the insurance latched onto that as a bit of a smoke screen to try to wriggle out of a big pay out, or whether it was a genuine mistake I don't think we will ever know. All that matters is that they came good in the end. Eventually!"

"Relatively speaking," I said darkly.

"True," he agreed. "They only covered part of the work, but at least it got us started, so that we could then help ourselves back onto our own feet."

"I suppose so." I nodded slowly. He was right, he had said it before. Perhaps now, having finally managed to process all that had happened, I was ready to listen.

"Even if we had had the accidental damage cover I bet it would have still been a long old haul to prove we qualified for that, simply because of the scope and complexity of the situation." He moved over to the desk as he spoke and leaned against it with his arms crossed, before continuing.

"The mistake we made, and please note I said WE, was to buy an old house. Not because it fell down although that obviously wasn't ideal let's face it, but because it was never going to fit into any of the standard definitions available when taking out house insurance policies."

"But..." I interrupted then stopped when he shook his head at me.

"I know! We took great care to choose a company that understands old properties. However, we were very naive to think that we were going to be fully covered against all eventualities. That was an unintentional miscalculation but we made it years before the actual cob collapse happened. Think about it! Elements of the house were very, very old, but bits of it were not quite so old and some of it was really new. We had part cob construction, part wood, some brick and glass and then finally some concrete all mixed in. It was thatched but also tiled with a section of conservatory roof too. It had an old chimney and also a second more modern chimney. I challenge anyone to find me one insurance company tick box form that will cover all of that, especially over the telephone."

"I should have tried harder." I insisted. "I should have thought of that. There must have been something I could have done to either stop it or fix it."

"Don't be ridiculous! Stop being such a control freak! I know you like to organise everything but sometimes it is just not possible. It was a disaster waiting to happen from the moment we bought the house. Accidental damage or not, the house was a ticking time bomb waiting for that one final winter when the biggest storms on record for 250 years simply blew it up."

"I guess," I conceded.

"Remember it could just as easily have been me that made the phone call to set up the insurance when we moved in. The result would have been the same."

"Really?"

He sighed, "I have said all this to you before you know and I will keep on saying it if I have to. Are you ready to listen to me now? Or are you going to carry on blaming yourself? You are so stressed all the time now. Worrying about everything and scared of your own shadow. I have been really worried about you. You are constantly convinced that the worst is about to happen and keep trying to work out ways to avoid potential disasters. It's an impossible task. You cannot micro-manage everything. You will make yourself ill. Don't forget that you risk damaging the rest of us as much as yourself by refusing to let it go."

He stepped over to me and slid his arms around me. "Please let it go?" he asked. I turned to face him resting my cheek on his chest. "I feel just as guilty as you, you know," he continued after a moment.

"Why?"

He sighed. "For loads of reasons. For not being able to afford to immediately move us all into a hotel or rent another property straight away. I should have been able to provide for the family. I should have worked harder, made better arrangements for emergencies."

"But you were working so hard already," I said, "and you did take on extra when you could. The house insurance we were paying was supposed to cover emergencies! For goodness sake it was costing us enough!"

"There you go, see? It's not just you that can play the unreasonable blame game. We have to relax. Carrying it with us will give it a power it doesn't deserve. It's over, let's move on without it. All of us. Together."

"OK." I leaned happily into a warm hug and smiled.

"I just have one question though," he said.

"What?" I asked suspiciously.

"Where the hell are we going to put all these paintings?"

Epilogue

Definition: A comment or conclusion from the author at the end of a book.

That, I think, is an appropriate place to leave our heroine wrapped as she is in the arms of her own, personal superhero. They have both reached a place of understanding, acceptance and forgiveness (however necessary or not – let's not start debating that one again) and are content to move forward into the future if not completely whole then as a partially repaired 'work-in-progress'.

After all who among us do not bear the scars of our past?

***

Now, a brief footnote on those we have abandoned in a crumbly cottage in the past.

Don't worry! The younger versions of our hero and heroine and their intrepid, happy, little band of Barbarian campers are going to be OK too!

It's Christmas and who needs more of a reason to celebrate?

There are fairy lights strung along the crazy paving to light the pathway from Hattie to the house. Skelly has been brought around from the front of the house and is now ensconced comfortably in a deck chair on the patio next to a Christmas tree in a pot. He is currently sporting a warm red cloak and a battered old top hat from a charity shop with some tinsel around the brim, whilst holding an empty beer can in celebration of the festive season.

It is time to draw this little tale to a close as the family contemplate their small success. They don't yet realise what a dangerous and rocky mountain road they still have to climb in their quest to rebuild their home and become their future selves, but that is another story. The insurance company have agreed a rudimentary package of help for them and this is the helping hand up that they so desperately need to start repairs. All the rest can be worked out in time. One step at a time!

It would be a shame to upset them, with knowledge of what is to come. So, for now let us allow them to look forward to their cosy little Christmas. A Christmas that would admittedly be rather light on actual presents but extremely weighted towards good company and excellent nourishment, with baked ham, roast turkey, pigs in blankets, buckets of cava, or lemonade, dependent on age, and 100's of chocolates on the Christmas tree. (Yes, yes, OK, there would also be Yorkshire pudding, stuffing, vegetables, brandy butter, mince pies, Christmas pudding, crackers with hats and terrible jokes and much, much more besides. Please stop being so literal!)

They don't know that they are not yet out of the woods but at this moment in time, it does not matter.

Should they have fought harder and not accepted the insurance company's bare minimum offer? Some would say yes. It could be suggested that they should have pushed for more comprehensive assistance but each delay would no doubt mean additional months and even potentially years in

Accidental Damage

limbo, probably with yet further assessments being carried out and reports being written but no restorative action taken.

It should be remembered that in all decisions our beleaguered couple have been motivated entirely by damage limitation, choosing the option that ensured that their beloved Barbarians would suffer the least. Thus any choice that would speed up the repair process and enable them to resume normal life had to be made, regardless of who was liable or responsible for the monetary bottom line.

The final rebuild job was still a massive financial gamble for our family. It meant that they would potentially lose the house anyway due to the huge debt that would inevitably need to be run up trying to fill the fiscal gaps in the final repair bill. The unavoidable conclusion of which being that the property would almost definitely need to be sold once fully repaired. Nevertheless the family would be safe and that is all that they care about.

So we shall leave the family there dear reader, as they are about to celebrate what was an unexpectedly wonderful crumbly-cottage-and-caravan-based family Christmas together.

The promised start date of the rebuild was set for the 2nd January. A new year filled with fresh possibilities (and no doubt more disasters knowing them but let us hush for now!).

Everything will be alright in the end.

Alice May

May you always have walls for the winds, a roof for the rain, tea beside the fire, laughter to cheer you and those you love near you...

Irish Blessing
Anon

The Comforting Recipes of Chaos and Logic

Crispy Cakes

Ingredients
To make this Crispy Cakes Recipe you will need:

1 x 100g bar milk or dark chocolate
90g/ (3 oz) rice crispies
12 small paper cake cases.

Method

Melt the chocolate in a bowl over a saucepan of simmering water. Once melted carefully remove the bowl from the saucepan.

Add the rice crispies and stir in to the chocolate mix until entirely covered in chocolate. Spoon, evenly, into the 12 paper cases.

Sprinkles on top make a really cheerful finishing touch.

Leave to cool in the fridge.

Chaos would like to remind you not to forget to scrape the bowl out thoroughly at the end though, as it is the cook's privilege. Although Logic does state that if you have small children or Barbarians on hand that you need to keep quiet, then it is acceptable to hand it over (assuming safe supervision of any glassware of course). Anything for a bit of peace!

Fridge Cake
Ingredients

250g (8oz) digestive biscuits or rich tea depending on preference
150g (5oz) milk chocolate
150g (5oz) dark chocolate
100g (3½oz) unsalted butter
150g (5oz) golden syrup
150g (5oz) raisins
Handful of mini marshmallows (optional)
Nuts are also optional but be careful with regard to any nut allergy sufferers among your guests.

Method

Use cling film to line a 20cm (8in) shallow, square-shaped tin. Leave additional cling film to hang over the sides.

Bash the biscuits into pieces using a rolling pin. Logic would dictate that you could put can them in a strong plastic bag first before hitting them with the rolling pin so they don't go everywhere! Or you could follow Chaos' method that involves just put the biscuits in a really large bowl before bashing down with the end of your rolling pin and simply enjoying the mess that ensues. I guess it rather depends how much time you have allocated for clearing up.

Melt chocolate, butter and golden syrup in a heatproof bowl set over a pan of simmering water. Stir occasionally.

Remove the bowl from the heat and stir in the broken biscuits, raisins and mini marshmallows (optional but really, really nice – makes it a bit like rocky road).

Spoon the mixture into the tin. Level the surface and press down.

Leave to cool, in the fridge for 1-2 hours to set.

Turn out the cake and peel off the cling film being careful not to miss any little bits. Logic respectfully reminds you that no one likes chomping through forgotten bits of old cling-film.

Cut into squares and enjoy.

Please note that Chaos invites you to believe her when she says that they won't last long, so you probably better double up on your ingredients next time you order on-line, save the delivery driver the extra trip.

Chocolate Chip Cookies

Ingredients

150g butter
160g sugar
1 large egg
220g plain flour
0.5 tsp bicarbonate soda
0.25 tsp salt
200g chocolate chips

Accidental Damage

Method

Preheat the oven to 190C/375F/Gas mark 5.

Melt the butter in a bowl, add sugar and beat in the eggs. Add the rest of the ingredients and mix well. Put a tablespoon of the mixture on a baking tray and back for 8-10 minutes to see how far it will spread during cooking. This will give you an idea how many you can cook on the tray in each batch without the dough running all over your lovely clean oven.

Logic would suggest lining your tray with baking paper but Chaos would ask why bother? Again it's got a lot to do with the cleaning up and how organised you are feeling I suppose.

Bake the remaining dough in batches until all is used. Then leave to cool for a few minutes before transferring to wire racks to cool further. Logic recommends this as they can break if moved too soon although Chaos maintains that the broken ones are testers for the cook to taste to ensure quality control. You can decide which method you concur with.

Personally I prefer to remain impartial, as long as my ready supply of biscuits continues why on earth would I step in?

Serve with a large cup of tea.

You deserve a break.

Innovative Games for Bored Barbarian Boys

Catch for ruffians

Equipment
1 large sheet of paper carefully scrumpled up into a tight ball, this could be newspaper, wrapping paper or simply an old envelope or empty crisp packet. (Even better use your older sister's A-level physics notes – such fun to see her reaction!)

1 room in your house. It is preferable to choose one where there are plenty of potentially breakable ornaments as this adds to the general excitement of the game.

2 or more ruffians. The more the merrier.

Rules of the game

Pass (throw really hard) the ball of paper systematically between you without dropping it.

Points are awarded for how close you can get to potentially breakable items without actually causing any damage.

Additional points are awarded as appropriate for the maximum possible annoyance that can be caused to any siblings choosing not to play.

NB: Please note that this is not a good activity to engage in if you wish to remain on good terms with your mother.

In door cricket for the very brave thug

Equipment

Much as outlined previously but please add a long cardboard tube as is generally found inside a roll of kitchen towels or even wrapping paper. (Feel free to unravel one that isn't finished yet and leave the unused paper lying around to get in the way. No one will mind.)

Rules of the game

You've seen cricket, it's much like that. Make it up as you go along. (Who needs rules?)

Changing the (non-existent) rules as you go along is an excellent way of winding up a participating sibling too.

Enjoy!

NB: see previous warning note. You really don't want to upset your mother.

Alice May

About the Author
Alice May

At 45 years old, Alice May is a working mother with four not-so-small children.

She is fortunate enough to be married to (probably) the most patient man on the planet and they live in, what used to be, a ramshackle old cottage in the country.

Her conservatory is always festooned with wet washing and her kitchen full of cake.

She loves listening to the radio.

Inspired by true-life events and fuelled by some really frantic painting sessions this story wouldn't leave her alone until it was written.

She hopes you enjoy it.

If you have any comments about this book please send them to: alicegmay@hotmail.com
Website: www.alicemay.weebly.com
Twitter: @AliceMay_Author
Or find Alice May's author page on Facebook.

P.S. Please note that no Barbarians were harmed during the writing of this book.

Printed in Poland
by Amazon Fulfillment
Poland Sp. z o.o., Wrocław